AT THE ME D0292504

A rifle crashed, but the hurried shot came nowhere near Longarm. He saw two men sitting on their horses about fifty feet upstream. One of them had already fired at him, and the other was trying to bring his rifle to bear while his companion jacked another shell into the Winchester's chamber. Longarm's rifle was on his saddle, and he wished he had it right now. He would just have to make do with the revolver . . .

Longarm threw himself backward and lifted the Colt, but this time the rider used his rifle in a different sort of attack. The barrel of the Winchester cracked across Longarm's right wrist, and he felt his fingers go numb. The Colt slipped out of his grasp . . .

DON'T MISS THESE
ALL-ACTION WESTERN SERIES
FROM THE BERKLEY PUBLISHING GROUP

THE GUNSMITH by J. R. Roberts
> Clint Adams was a legend among lawmen, outlaws, and ladies. They called him . . . the Gunsmith.

LONGARM by Tabor Evans
> The popular long-running series about U.S. Deputy Marshal Long—his life, his loves, his fight for justice.

LONE STAR by Wesley Ellis
> The blazing adventures of Jessica Starbuck and the martial arts master, Ki. Over eight million copies in print.

SLOCUM by Jake Logan
> Today's longest-running action Western. John Slocum rides a deadly trail of hot blood and cold steel.

TABOR EVANS

LONGARM

AND THE
DRIFTING BADGE

JOVE BOOKS, NEW YORK

LONGARM AND THE DRIFTING BADGE

A Jove Book / published by arrangement with
the author

PRINTING HISTORY
Jove edition / May 1994

ISBN: 0-515-11375-1

A JOVE BOOK®
Jove Books are published by The Berkley Publishing Group,
200 Madison Avenue, New York, New York 10016.
JOVE and the "J" design are trademarks
belonging to Jove Publications, Inc.

PRINTED IN THE UNITED STATES OF AMERICA

10 9 8 7 6 5 4 3 2 1

Chapter 1

It was just his luck, Longarm thought as he bellied down in the mud next to the water trough and listened to the bullets thudding into it, to wander into the middle of a shootout when he didn't even know who the hell was trying to kill him.

He raised up enough to throw a couple of slugs at the gents across the street who were shooting at him. There was no time to see if he'd hit anything, because another volley came his way and made him duck down again.

If this didn't beat all!

Here he'd ridden into this fly-specked cow town called La Junta on routine business, and no sooner had he swung down from the saddle than folks had started shooting at him. He drew a deep, exasperated breath, spit out some mud, and waited for another lull in the shooting.

"Be careful, Marshal!" somebody yelled.

For an instant, Longarm thought they were hollering at him. After all, he carried the badge and identification papers of a deputy United States marshal, and as many people called him "Marshal" as they did "Deputy." But then he realized that somebody else had taken cards in this hand. More gunshots came from down the street, and somebody yelped in pain

1

inside the building across from Longarm where the bush-whackers were holed up.

Longarm stuck his head out long enough to see a man running diagonally across the street toward his position behind the water trough. The newcomer wasn't charging Longarm, though. The gun in his hand spat fire and lead toward the building across the street, and Longarm knew this stranger was on his side. A second later, he saw the afternoon sun flash on something pinned to the man's vest and recognized him for a fellow lawman. That was probably a town marshal's badge he wore.

Bullets kicked up dust around the boot heels of the local star-packer. The man threw himself behind a buckboard parked at the hitch rack about ten yards down the street from the water trough Longarm was using for cover. The wagon team was nervous—justifiably so considering all the lead that was flying around—and the horses might just pull loose and bolt. Longarm was glad he was behind the water trough; at least it wasn't going to run off and leave him exposed.

The La Junta lawman knelt behind the buckboard and fired a couple of times at the men across the street, then crouched lower and called over to Longarm, "You all right, mister?"

"So far," Longarm replied. "What in blazes is going on here?"

"Bank robbery. You just sit tight. I'll get you out of that spot."

Longarm wasn't in the habit of other people having to pull his fat out of the fire. He called back, "I'm a lawman myself. I'll give you a hand with those bank-robbing rascals."

The town marshal grinned across at Longarm and said, "Always glad to work with a fellow officer." Then he leaned out and squeezed off a couple of shots at the forted-up bank robbers.

Longarm tried to remember the layout of this settlement on the Ogallala Trail along the Kansas-Colorado line. He had never been to La Junta until today, and he hadn't been paying that much attention when he rode in. As best he could recall, the bank was on the opposite side of the street, a couple of doors down from the building where the bandits had holed up. In the brief glimpse of the place Longarm had gotten before he went diving for cover, the building had looked to him like some sort of abandoned store.

"There a back door in that place?" he asked the local law.

The man nodded. "There is, but it's boarded up on the outside."

"They could bust through."

The town marshal shook his head. "I sent some of the townsmen around back to cover the door with rifles. Besides, the gang's horses are out front here. They wouldn't get far on foot."

That made sense to Longarm. He chanced another look over the top of the water trough, and saw the half-dozen or so horses tied up at the hitch rack on the other side of the street. They were as skittish as the wagon team, and with good cause.

A glance up and down the street told Longarm that every-body else had wisely sought cover. A bullet had no way of knowing if the person it was about to hit was guilty or innocent, so when shooting broke out, most folks had sense enough to hunt a hole and stay put. It was left to men like him and the local law to face the guns of the badmen.

Oh, well, Longarm sighed. He knew the job was dangerous when he took it.

He emptied his Colt at the abandoned store across the street, then hunkered down again and started thumbing fresh cartridges into the .44. The town marshal was doing the same thing behind the buckboard. The shots from across the street were slowing down a little, and Longarm wondered if the outlaws were running low on ammunition. He sure as hell hoped so. He pure-dee hated standoffs like this. The best

3

solution would be for the bandits to run out of bullets and surrender.

The horses attached to the wagon were pulling harder on their reins now and giving out frantic whickers of fear. They were going to bolt soon, Longarm knew. He called out to the marshal, "I'll cover you while you find a better spot."

The man shook his head. "Hell with that," he snapped. "I'm tired of this."

And with that, he darted out from behind the wagon and ran straight toward the building where the outlaws were holed up. The pistol in his hand boomed as fast as he could cock it and pull the trigger.

"Crazy son of a bitch!" Longarm exclaimed as he surged up from behind the water trough and opened up on the building. The other lawman was going to get himself killed with a damnfool stunt like this. Longarm started to duck behind the trough again and let the marshal get shot to ribbons, but he couldn't do that. Not and live with himself afterwards.

He did the only thing he could. He joined the charge.

Letting out a yell like a soldier going into battle, Longarm ran across the street, sending bullets punching through the front wall of the building as his boots thudded against the hard-packed dirt. The local lawman had reached the boardwalk on the other side of the street by now, seemingly untouched by the bullets coming from the building. He crashed into the front door and burst through it, vanishing into the building as he tumbled through the opening. Longarm heard more shots racketing in there.

As he bounded onto the boardwalk, Longarm saw movement through a window that had had all the glass shot out of it. A gent in a duster was standing there and twisting back and forth as if he couldn't make up his mind who to shoot at. Longarm saved him the bother of making a decision by putting a .44 slug through the Bull Durham tag that dangled out of his shirt pocket. The man crumpled and Longarm went diving through the window, feeling more than a little like a fool.

He hit the floor hard amid shards of glass and rolled over, then came up in a crouch and lifted his gun. There was nobody left to shoot at, though. The outlaws were sprawled around the dusty floor in various attitudes of death, and the La Junta marshal was calmly reloading his gun.

"Thanks for getting that last one," he said dryly to Longarm. "Saved me some trouble."

Longarm straightened and brushed splinters of glass off the knees of his trousers with his free hand. Part of him wanted to yell at the local law for taking such foolhardy chances and putting them both in even more danger, but that could wait. First he wanted to check the bank robbers.

They were all dead except for one man who stared up at Longarm with bloody froth on his lips and air sucking through the bullet holes in his chest. He wasn't going to last long, but he was still conscious and aware enough of his surroundings to look at Longarm with hate in his eyes.

With a frown of surprise, Longarm realized he recognized the more-than-half-dead young outlaw. "Damn it, Hobie," he said as he knelt beside the man, "I figured you to have more sense than to hook up with a bunch of bank robbers. Thought that stretch behind bars might've done you some good."

The mortally wounded outlaw coughed and grimaced at the pain filling him up. "Reckon you should've . . . known better . . . Long. Once a fella . . . crosses the line . . . there ain't no chance—"

That was all he got out before another shudder ran through him and his eyes glazed over in death. Grim-faced, Longarm straightened and let out a sigh.

"Friend of yours?"

The question came from the local law. Longarm turned toward him and shook his head. "Just a young cowpoke I arrested a while back for trying to hold up a stagecoach. He botched that job too, and didn't make off with a cent of loot.

5

He'd never been in trouble before, so the judge gave him a pretty light sentence. Reckon it didn't take."

"I wouldn't waste my sympathy on scum like that. He'd've gunned you down without a second thought. In fact, I was down the street when the shooting started. That fella fired first, and it was you he was aiming at. What do you think about that?"

"Hobie must've recognized me as a lawman and panicked," Longarm muttered. "There hadn't been any shooting before that?"

"Nope, but I'd already spotted 'em and was working my way down the street so's I'd be closer before I braced 'em. That youngster just opened the ball a little earlier than I'd planned, that's all." The town lawman had holstered his revolver, and now he stuck out his hand. "Frank Nemo. I'm the marshal of La Junta."

Longarm slipped his own Colt back into its cross-draw rig and shook hands with Nemo. "Name's Custis Long," he said. "deputy U.S. marshal out of the Denver office."

Nemo grinned. "Sure, you must work for Billy Vail."

"You know ol' Billy?"

"Nope, never met the man. But I remember his name from the wire he sent me saying that one of his deputies would be coming out this way."

"That's right, I'm here to pick up Jack Paige." Longarm reached inside his coat. "I've got the prisoner release papers here somewhere . . ."

"Never mind that now," Nemo said. "I imagine you want to get cleaned up first."

Longarm looked down at his mud-splattered brown tweed coat and pants. His vest was covered with mud too. Most of the street outside was dry, but the area around the water trough that he had chosen for shelter had been muddy and churned up by hooves. The team attached to that buckboard had probably been watered there not long before.

"I wouldn't mind, at that," admitted Longarm. "I've got some clean clothes in my saddlebags."

"Well, why don't you go on over to Ramsey's Barber Shop? You can clean up and change your duds there, get those boots cleaned at the same time."

Longarm nodded. He'd had just about enough of this abandoned store. The place had probably smelled pretty musty to start with, what with being closed up for a while, and half a dozen dead outlaws scattered around the room didn't freshen things up any.

"I'll take care of this bunch," Nemo went on. "I imagine somebody's already sent for the undertaker."

"I'll be down to your office directly," Longarm told him.

"Anybody in town can show you the way," Nemo said with a grin. "Ramsey's is on the other side of the street, four doors down."

"Thanks." Longarm went to the doorway and paused to look back and say, "That was an . . . unexpected play, Marshal, charging the place like you did."

Nemo's wide grin didn't budge. "Can't cut these outlaws any slack, Marshal Long. You got to take the fight to 'em. But I reckon a man like you knows that already."

Longarm inclined his head and didn't say one way or the other. But as he headed across the street toward Ramsey's Barber Shop, he thought that he was damned glad he didn't have to side with Marshal Frank Nemo all the time. That would be a good way to get himself killed.

As Nemo had said, Longarm had no trouble finding his office a little later. He'd put on his spare trousers and vest and brushed as much of the mud off his coat as he could. Luckily, the stuff hadn't splattered on his shirt or the snuff-brown, flat-crowned hat. The stovepipe boots he wore had been cleaned up by Ramsey's bootblack. Longarm was still a mite upset that Hobie Carson hadn't gone straight, but he knew from experience that he couldn't worry about every kid who turned owlhoot. If he tried, he'd have gone crazy in a hurry.

The street was a lot more crowded now that the gunplay was over. The first man Longarm asked pointed out the marshal's office to him, and Longarm ambled down the boardwalk toward the stone building, tipping his hat to the sun-bonneted ladies he passed. Some of them he looked twice at, and got a few flirtatious smiles in return. For a trail town, La Junta looked fairly settled and prosperous, and Longarm might not have minded spending more time there if he hadn't had a prisoner to get back to Denver.

He opened the door of the combined marshal's office and jail and stepped inside. The dim interior was cool after the heat of the late afternoon. The season might be getting on toward fall, but the days were still quite warm.

The town marshal's office looked like a hundred others Longarm had seen. There was an old wooden desk, a broken-down sofa, gun racks on the walls, a couple of filing cabinets, and a cast-iron stove in the corner with a pot of coffee simmering on it. An open door in the wall behind the desk led to a cell block. Longarm glanced through the door but couldn't see any prisoners from where he was. He nodded to Frank Nemo, who sat at the desk with his chair tipped back and his boot heels resting on the scarred surface.

Nemo had taken off his hat, revealing a shock of hair that had started out sand-colored but was mostly gray now. Longarm had pegged his age as early forties. Nemo wore a shirt that had once been red but had faded to a sort of pale rose, a leather vest, and denim pants. He gave Longarm a friendly grin and said, "I see Ramsey took care of you."

"Wanted to give me a shave and splash some bay rum on me too, but I didn't have the time. I want to get back to Denver with Paige as soon as I can."

Nemo let down the front legs of his chair and sat up straight, clasping his knobby-knuckled hands together on the desk in front of him. "Well, now, that's going to be a problem, Marshal

8

Long. You see, Jack Paige isn't here anymore."

Longarm stiffened. It had been less than a week since Nemo had contacted Billy Vail's office to let him know that a fugitive wanted on a federal warrant had been apprehended in La Junta. Vail had wired back immediately, saying that he would send a man to pick up the prisoner. Longarm was that man.

And now Nemo was claiming that Paige was gone. With a frown, Longarm asked, "You got any idea where he is?"

"I know exactly where he is," replied Nemo. "He's buried in the town's potter's field."

That news took Longarm even more by surprise. "Paige is dead?" he asked somewhat redundantly.

"He tried to escape," Nemo said. "I had to gun him. He didn't give me any choice, Marshal."

The words were calm and matter-of-fact, one lawman reporting on a situation to another lawman. But something struck Longarm as wrong. He'd looked over the paperwork Billy Vail had given him before starting this job, and something about it didn't jibe.

He dug the documents out of an inside coat pocket and spread them out on the desk in front of Nemo. "That description fit the fella you had in your jail, Marshal?" he asked, pointing to the appropriate section on the federal warrant.

Nemo scanned the description and nodded. "That was him, all right. No doubt about it. And he never denied being Jack Paige."

Longarm's frown deepened. "Paige was wanted on charges connected to some water rights scandal back in Pennsylvania. Don't seem to be the sort of desperado who'd shoot it out with a lawman."

"A man can change once he's been out here on the frontier for a while. Seems to me like there were some state warrants on him too . . ." Nemo opened a drawer in the desk and dug around in it. He produced several reward dodgers and tossed them on top of the documents Longarm had brought

9

with him. "He was wanted for theft and suspicion of stealing a horse. Looks like he hardened up some since leaving Pennsylvania."

"Well, maybe," Longarm said. He had to admit that sometimes men who had been involved in petty crime back east had become major outlaws after crossing the Mississippi. Anyway, Nemo had no reason to lie about what had happened, as far as Longarm could see.

"I'm sorry, Marshal," the local lawman said. "I reckon you came all this way for nothing. I would've wired Denver and told them not to bother sending anybody, but I figured it was already too late to stop you when it happened."

"When was that?"

"Day before yesterday."

Longarm nodded. He was already on the trail by then, just as Nemo had thought. He pulled up one of the chairs in front of the desk, reversed it and straddled it, and slipped a couple of cheroots from the pocket of his vest. With obvious pleasure, Nemo took the one that Longarm extended across the desk to him. When both men had their smokes going, Longarm asked, "What happened, exactly? If you don't mind my asking, that is."

"Don't mind at all," Nemo answered without hesitation. "Paige jumped me when I brought him his supper. My mistake, really, since I was alone in the office at the time, but he hadn't given any trouble so far." Nemo waved his cheroot at the federal and local warrants on the desk. "And you can see for yourself that he didn't have any sort of reputation as a dangerous badman. But he'd managed to loosen the leg of his bunk and pry it off, and he walloped me with it when I wasn't expecting anything. Didn't knock me out or kill me, though, and that was his mistake. He just clouted me, and when I fell down he grabbed my gun out of my holster and ran. Figure he thought he could make it out the front and grab a horse."

"But he didn't," Longarm said.

"I yelled for him to stop and went after him. I grabbed one of the rifles off the rack there"—Nemo jerked a thumb over his shoulder at the rifle rack on the wall behind him, next to the cell block door—"and yelled at him again just as he reached the front door. He turned around and pointed my own gun at me." Nemo's face hardened. "I didn't like that. No, sir, not one bit. Drilled him before he could shoot."

"You keep loaded rifles on the wall?"

"An unloaded rifle don't come in very handy in a pinch, now does it?" Nemo grinned again, then became more solemn once more. "I didn't want to shoot him, Marshal Long, I truly didn't. But you know how it is when somebody's about to take a shot at you. Besides, I don't cotton to letting prisoners escape without putting up a fight."

"Can't blame you for that," Longarm agreed. He put his hands on his knees, shoved himself to his feet, and reached for the documents he had brought with him. As he stowed them away, he said, "I'll take these back to Denver and let my boss dispose of 'em however he sees fit. I don't expect anybody else'll have to bother you about Paige."

"No bother," Nemo said.

"Local coroner hold an inquest?"

Nemo nodded and said, "Sure. Verdict was a justifiable killing in the line of duty. Just like the hearing'll turn out when we get around to holding one on those sons of bitches we had to kill earlier today."

"You don't need me to stay around for that, do you?" Longarm asked, suddenly wary of being stuck there in La Junta for several days. Earlier he had thought he wouldn't mind spending some time there, but that had been pure speculation. In truth, he was just too damned fiddle-footed to sit around doing nothing for any length of time.

"No, I reckon you can go on back to Denver any time you want, especially if you write up a little statement for me about what happened today."

"I'll do that," Longarm promised. "As late as it is now, I might as well get me a room in the hotel and start back in the morning. That'll give me a chance to write up that statement for you this evening."

"The Sanders House is the best hotel in town," Nemo told him. "Tell 'em I sent you."

"I'll do that." Longarm held out his hand to Nemo. "Well, Marshal, I'm sorry we couldn't do business, I guess you could say."

Nemo shook hands with him. "Maybe another time."

Longarm nodded and left the office. He untied his horse from the hitch rack where he had left it when he first came into town, then led it to the nearest livery stable. Once the animal was taken care of, he toted his McClellan saddle and its attached saddle boot with the Winchester in it back down the street to the Sanders House. Marshal Nemo's name made the clerk hop to give Longarm a good room, right enough.

Longarm left the saddle and rifle in the hotel room, ate supper in the Sanders House dining room, then had a few drinks in the Alamo Saloon across the street. There were no fights or shootings or knifings while he was in the saloon. The girls working the barroom were all right but nothing special, Longarm decided, and anyway, he was tired. After a while he went back to the hotel, smoked one last cheroot as he used some of the hotel writing paper to scrawl that statement Nemo wanted, then undressed and stretched his powerful but weary frame out on the bed.

Except for that shootout with the would-be bank robbers, he thought just before he drifted off to sleep, this trip looked to be not only unnecessary but boring as well. He'd be glad to get back to Denver.

Chapter 2

Frank Nemo was in his office when Longarm stopped by there the next morning to give him the statement concerning the shootout with the bank robbers. Nemo barely glanced at the paper before dropping it on his desk. "That'll be fine," he assured Longarm. "I've never have been one to concern myself overmuch about all the paperwork that comes with carrying a badge. Always figured there were more important things to worry about."

"Sounds like we agree about that, Marshal," Longarm said. "I reckon I'll be heading back to Denver now if there's nothing else you need me for."

"Nothing official, but how about a bite of breakfast? Have you eaten yet?"

Longarm nodded. "Took my breakfast in the Sanders House dining room, but thanks anyway. I'll go on down to the livery stable and get my horse."

Nemo stood up and stuck his hand out. "Any time you get back over this way," he said, "you be sure and stop in, Deputy Long."

"I'll do that." Longarm shook hands with the man, then gave him a casual wave as he went out the door. Except for that tendency toward recklessness Nemo had displayed in charging the bank robbers, Longarm liked the marshal. And he'd been accused a time or two of being a mite reckless himself, so he couldn't very well hold that against Nemo either. He didn't expect his duties to bring him back to La Junta anytime soon, but you could never tell about things like that.

The hostler at the livery stable saddled up Longarm's horse and led the animal out of the barn. Longarm settled up his bill, getting a receipt so that he could turn it over to Henry, Billy Vail's clerk, and rode out of La Junta, his body rested and his mind at ease.

He headed west across the plains toward Denver. It was all flatland around here, rolling prairie that stretched all the way to the Front Range halfway across the state. A man could make good time, especially at this time of year. He didn't have to cross the Ogallala Trail itself, which ran just to the east of La Junta, right along the border between Kansas and Colorado. The government had opened up the trail earlier in the year, Longarm recalled, to give drovers an alternate route to the railroads. Kansas was a pretty civilized place now, and a lot of the settlers there had gotten proddy about allowing herds of longhorns to be driven across their land. The East still needed beef, though, and the Ogallala Trail let the Texas ranchers bypass Kansas almost entirely and drive their cattle straight to the railroad at Ogallala, Nebraska. Longarm had been over this way on assignments a time or two in the past, and he was glad he hadn't had to tangle with any trail herds this time.

Which wasn't to say there weren't any cattle around here. The plains were dotted with the grazing beasts. There were several massive ranches here in eastern Colorado, running thousands of head on their range. As Longarm kept the horse at an easy gait, the miles rolling past beneath them, he saw plenty of stock in the distance and men on horseback tending to them.

Along about noon, when Longarm was thinking about finding a nice shady spot under some scrub cottonwoods that lined the creeks in these parts and having some lunch, he spotted smoke rising into the sky ahead of him. Not enough smoke to signify any sort of trouble, he decided, but enough to poke his curiosity awake. Might be a cow camp up there, he thought, and if that was the case, the waddies who built the fire would no doubt be willing to share their son-of-a-bitch stew and pot of Arbuckle's.

He saw four cowhands as he drew nearer. All of them were afoot, but three horses and a wagon team were tied to some scrub brush nearby. The men had a good-sized fire going, and as Longarm rode up, he saw the handles of several branding irons sticking up, the other ends resting in the flames. There were no calves around at the moment, though, so these gents were obviously a branding crew waiting for other riders to sweep the countryside and bring them any stock that had missed being branded during the spring roundup.

"Howdy," called one of the cowboys as Longarm brought his horse to a stop. "Light and set a spell, stranger. We were just about to have some grub, and we'd be pleased if you'd join us."

"Much obliged," Longarm replied, nodding as he swung down from the saddle and tied the reins to another bush, not getting his mount too close to the cow ponies so that there wouldn't be any nipping or kicking between them.

The spokesman for the group extended a gloved hand. "I'm Tom Coffee," he said, "ramrod o' this outfit."

"Custis Long." The lawman left it at that, not explaining that the years and his profession had whittled his handle down to Longarm as far as most folks were concerned.

Tom Coffee was a stocky, broad-shouldered man with a wide, friendly, sun-bronzed face underneath a broad-brimmed, high-crowned white hat. He wore gloves, leather cuffs, and shotgun chaps, and a Colt Peacemaker with well-worn walnut grips rode in a holster on his right hip. He turned and indicated the men with him, saying, "These are some of my boys—Otto Barnes, Ignacio Castillo, and Ben LeDoux."

"Ride for one of the spreads around here, do you?" Longarm asked as he walked next to Coffee over to the cookfire, which was smaller than the branding fire.

"That's right, the Circle K. You know it?"

Longarm shook his head. "Can't say as I do, but I'm just passing through these parts, heading to Denver."

"Got business there, do you?"

Longarm nodded without elaborating, and Coffee seemed satisfied with the answer. Out here, a man could be friendly and gregarious by nature, but he still didn't press a stranger for too much information. It was just a matter of habit.

There was a pot of stew simmering over the low flames of the cookfire, along with a tin coffeepot sitting in the embers on the edge. Tom Coffee turned back one corner of the canvas that was tied over the bed of the ranch wagon, and dug around in the gear until he found an extra cup, which he filled and handed to Longarm. "There you go," he said. "I brew up the best pot of Arbuckle's around here, as I reckon you'd figure from my name."

"Didn't want to say anything about it," Longarm replied with a grin. "I figured you'd already heard all the jokes anybody could make out of it."

"And then some, twice over," Coffee chuckled. He filled his own cup, then waved at the ground next to the fire. "Pull up a chair."

"Don't mind if I do." Longarm sank down cross-legged on the ground while one of the other cowboys—the one called Barnes, Longarm thought—filled bowls with stew from the pot and passed them around.

Longarm had cowboyed some himself in his younger days, when he'd first drifted west after the Civil War, and he remembered well the good feeling of sitting around a campfire with some compadres and enjoying a respite from the never-ending work. That feeling came back to him now as he shared the meal with Coffee, Barnes, Castillo, and LeDoux. They were all friendly enough, although Coffee was by far the most talkative. From his soft accent, Longarm placed him as a Southerner, and that was confirmed when the man asked, "Did you get to take a hand in the War for the Southern Confederacy, Custis?"

"I was part of it, but I sort of disremember which side I wound up on, if you get my drift."

Coffee laughed and nodded. "I sure do. That was a long time ago, and I don't hold no grudges. Otto there was a Pennsylvania boy, so we might've shot at each other at Gettysburg. Don't make no never mind now. We've fought drought and floods and blizzards and Indians and cow thieves together, and that's what counts, ain't it, Otto?"

"Yah," the blond cowboy agreed. "We're pards, Tom."

"Damn right we are," Coffee said. "And Nacho's a god-damned Mex, o' course, but we get along just fine."

Ignacio Castillo grinned widely and said, "Until the night when I slit your throat, gringo. And you will never know when to expect that."

Coffee threw back his head and laughed. Evidently his insults and the Mexican's threats were a long-running joke. At least Longarm hoped they were. He liked Coffee too much to think about the man waking up some morning with a second mouth carved into his neck.

Nobody else seemed bothered by the exchange, though, so Longarm decided not to be either. He had plenty of cheroots in his pockets, since he had stocked up before leaving Denver on the assignment that had taken him to La Junta, so when the meal was over he handed smokes around to the other four men.

"Waiting for some other hands to bring in calves for branding?" he asked when all of them had puffed their cheroots into life.

17

Coffee nodded. "That's right."

"Never cared much for branding chores myself. I'd rather be out riding, and the stink of burned hide gets to a man after a while."

"True enough," admitted Coffee. "Somebody's got to do it, though."

"You're right about that." Longarm stood up, stretching to unkink his muscles. "Well, that was mighty enjoyable, gents, and I thank you for the grub. I'd best be moving on. I want to cover quite a few more miles before night catches me."

"Good luck to you, Custis," Coffee said as he stood up and shook hands once more with Longarm. The other three punchers gave him friendly waves as he moved to his horse, untied the reins, and mounted up. Longarm wheeled the horse around and heeled it into a trot, heading west again.

That had been a pleasant enough way to pass some time. Almost too pleasant, in fact. He could have easily stretched out underneath a tree, tipped his hat down over his eyes, and snoozed for an hour or two. A part of his brain argued that he should do just that. He'd get back to Denver soon enough. Billy Vail wasn't going to be happy that the prisoner he'd sent Longarm after had turned up dead, even though it wasn't Longarm's fault by any stretch of the imagination. No sense in hurrying just so he could listen to Billy fuss, Longarm reasoned.

He had gone several miles, leaving the little cow camp far behind, when he saw a spot that he just couldn't resist. A creek had cut a shallow gully in the plains, with gentle banks and a few trees and some brush growing alongside the stream. Longarm rode down the easy slope, dismounted, and let the horse drink its fill at the creek, then hobbled the animal so it wouldn't run off. That wasn't very likely even without the hobbles, Longarm thought. There was good grass along the creek, and the horse would probably be content to graze for a while without wandering.

Longarm got a drink himself, topped off his canteen with creek water, and then crawled under a bush for that nap. It was shady but warm here in this little bower, and he dozed off quickly.

He had no idea how long he had slept when he woke up suddenly, but he knew something was wrong. Senses and instincts that had been honed to a razor-keenness by years of living dangerously had roused him from his nap. Longarm remained perfectly still, however, his only movement the opening of his eyes to narrow slits.

Sunlight still slanted through the leaves and branches of the trees and brush, throwing a dappled pattern of light and shade on him. Longarm had a feeling not much time had passed since he had gone to sleep, half an hour maybe. Slowly, he turned his head one way and then the other, but he saw nothing up or down the creek to alarm him. The horse was still grazing along the bank about twenty feet away, but nothing else living was in sight except some birds hopping around in the trees.

Suddenly, the horse lifted its head sharply, ears pricking forward. It had smelled or heard something, Longarm knew, and a second later he heard noises himself. The steady sound of hoofbeats grew louder as several riders drew closer.

They weren't in a hurry, though. Judging by what Longarm could hear, they were just ambling along, maybe following the creek. The presence of the riders didn't *have* to signify any kind of threat.

But then in the next moment, Longarm heard the riders talking to each other and didn't like what they were saying.

"Where do you reckon he got off to?"

"Damned if I know. If you hadn't lost his tracks—"

"Horses and cattle go across here all the time! A goddamned Apache couldn't follow sign around here."

"Keep your voice down. He could be around here somewhere, and we don't want to warn him."

There was no way for Longarm to know if they were talking about him or somebody else. One thing he was sure of, though: They didn't have anything good in mind for whomever they were looking for. He didn't recognize either voice, but that didn't mean much. At least there were only two of them . . . or two that he had heard so far anyway.

The horses were louder now, and Longarm knew they were getting closer. If it hadn't been for his mount, he might have been able to lie there under the bush and let the riders go on by unaware of his presence. At any moment, though, they were going to spot his mount—

"Hey, look there! That's the horse he was ridin'!"

Longarm heard the unmistakable metallic shuttling sound of a Winchester lever being worked. "Come on," the other man said. "Let's get down there and look for him. We'll teach him to horn in where he ain't wanted!"

Well, there was no doubt it now, Longarm thought as the two riders sent their horses crashing through the brush alongside the creek. He was the one they were after, although he had no idea why. He could tell from the sounds that they were still off to his right, so he rolled left, palming out the .44 from the cross-draw rig as he moved.

There was no way to stand up without making some noise, and as Longarm came to his feet, one of the men searching for him yelled, "There he is!"

A rifle crashed, but the hurried shot came nowhere near Longarm. He saw two men sitting on their horses about fifty feet upstream. One of them had already fired at him, and the other was trying to bring his rifle to bear while his companion jacked another shell into the Winchester's chamber. Longarm's rifle was on his saddle, and he wished he had it right now. He would just have to make do with the revolver.

He squeezed off a shot and saw one of the men jolt in the saddle, then sag forward. A groan came from the man as he dropped his rifle. The other one got off a shot, though, clipping a branch only a foot or so from Longarm, who dived to the side and down. The brush wouldn't stop a .44–40 slug, but at least it would conceal him for a few seconds.

"You bastard! You killed Mitch!"

With that angry shout, the man drove his horse forward through the brush. Longarm scuttled to one side, the toes of his boots digging into the sandy soil along the creek bank as he kept his balance with his free hand. As it was, he was almost too slow. The horseman was suddenly right on top of him, and Longarm had to go down and roll desperately to avoid the slashing hooves.

The rifle blasted again, the slug kicking grit into Longarm's face. The sand burned his eyes and made the world blur crazily before him. He triggered a couple of shots, more as a distraction than anything else, as he swiped at his eyes with his free hand and tried to clear his vision.

The horse loomed up over him again. Longarm threw himself backward and lifted the Colt, but this time the rider used his rifle in a different sort of attack. The barrel of the Winchester cracked across Longarm's right wrist, and he felt his fingers go numb. The Colt slipped out of his grasp.

With a quick, backhanded motion, the rider slammed the rifle barrel against Longarm's head, sending the lawman's hat spinning away. Longarm slumped to the ground, fireworks exploding behind his eyes. He knew that if he lost consciousness, there was a good chance he would never wake up. The part of his brain that could still work shouted at him to hang on.

"Get up. Get up, you son of a bitch!" The rider was off his horse now, standing next to Longarm, kicking him painfully in the side with sharp-toed boots. The blows thudded into Longarm and rolled him along the ground next to the creek. "Time to pay now for what you done!"

Longarm hadn't done *anything* as far as he could remember, not today anyway. He had plenty of enemies, though, and in fact only the day before he had unwittingly ruined the bank robbery being committed by Hobie Carson and his pards. Could be not all of the gang had come into La Junta to pull the job. Some of them could have hung back and stayed out of town, just in case there was trouble.

That made sense, all right, but Longarm suddenly realized he was wasting time thinking while he was getting the hell stomped out of him. He twisted on the ground as the man launched another kick at him, but this one didn't land. As the booted foot whipped past him, Longarm reached up, grabbed hold of it, and heaved as hard as he could.

The man went over backward with a startled yell. Longarm's head was swimming from the blow with the rifle and his muscles obeyed only sluggishly, but he forced himself to go after his attacker. He knocked the rifle aside, out of the man's grasp, and started slugging him in the face.

Arching his back, the man threw Longarm off to the side. Some of Longarm's strength had come back to him now, though, and he was able to roll over and surge back to his feet in time to meet the rush as the man came at him. The straight punch that Longarm threw had all of his power behind it, and the man ran right into the blow. He went backward like he had slammed into a wall, stumbling over his own feet until he fell back into the shallow creek.

Longarm landed on top of him, grappling for a hold. One of the man's hands came out of the water holding a knife, and Longarm grabbed his wrist just in time to hold back the blade. With his other hand, he found the man's neck and clamped his fingers around it in a vise-like grip. The man started to thrash, throwing water high into the air as he flailed around.

Gradually, the man's strength began to desert him as Longarm held his head under the surface of the creek. With his other hand, Longarm pushed the man's knife arm back, and after a couple of minutes the hand holding the knife relaxed and the weapon slipped away to fall into the water with a small splash. The man was limp now, and Longarm didn't know if he was dead or merely unconscious. He didn't really give a damn which it was either.

Pushing himself farther up on the creek bank, Longarm hauled the body out of the water. Dead, all right, he saw as he tried to gulp down enough air to ease the heaving of his chest and the pounding in his head. He'd come close to dying himself, here beside this peaceful prairie stream. Too damned close.

Longarm took a better look at the dead man's face. Even with the features twisted and frozen in death, Longarm knew he'd never seen the man before. It was bad enough when people he knew tried to kill him, but to have perfect strangers wanting him dead was downright discouraging.

He pushed himself to his feet and looked around. There was still another man unaccounted for, although Longarm knew he'd ventilated the son of a bitch with his first shot. Pushing through the brush, Longarm headed upstream.

The second man was nowhere to be seen.

Longarm's nerves prickled, and he sensed the rustle of brush behind him before he actually heard it. He threw himself forward, digging for the derringer hidden in his vest pocket as he fell. A gun blasted somewhere close to him.

He rolled over and brought out the .44-caliber derringer, which was attached to the gold-link chain that had his Ingersoll pocket watch on the other end. The deadly little two-shot weapon had saved his bacon on more than one occasion, and it did so again now as the wounded man charged toward him, yelling and firing a pistol. Longarm pushed himself up into a sitting position and triggered the derringer.

The bullet smacked into the chest of the onrushing man and tumbled him off his feet to land face down. Longarm scrambled upright again and ran over to the man, keeping the derringer trained on him as he approached. The man had

23

dropped his revolver, though, and was making no effort to recover it.

Longarm knelt beside the man, grasped his shoulder, and rolled him over. There was some blood on his chest where the bullet from the derringer had hit him, but the shirt around his midsection was sodden with the stuff. Longarm knew he'd gut-shot the man the first time without really meaning to. There hadn't been enough time to place his bullet so precisely.

The man's eyelids flickered open, and he stared accusingly up at Longarm. "You . . . you've kilt me, you bastard!" he gasped.

"Seemed to be the thing to do at the time, old son," Longarm told him, his voice cool but not too harsh. The threat was over. "Why were you and your pard gunning for me anyway?"

"You . . . you know . . . you saw . . ."

Longarm didn't recognize this man either, so he played the hunch he'd had earlier. "Saw Hobie Carson, is that what you're trying to say? Hell, I wasn't paying any attention back there in La Junta until Hobie took a shot at me. If he hadn't lost his head, I might not have ever noticed . . ."

He stopped in mid-sentence when he saw how the man's eyes had turned to glass. He was talking to a corpse, and that was just a waste of breath. With a sigh, Longarm stood up.

He found his Colt, made sure the barrel wasn't fouled, and holstered it after reloading the empty chambers. When he had done the same with the derringer, he caught the horses that the men had been riding. He could sling the bodies over the saddles and tote them back to Denver, he thought, but that would take a couple of days yet, and by the time he got there those boys wouldn't exactly be nosegays. Better to plant them right here, even if it did mean he'd have to dig a hole.

That was what he did, after checking their pockets to see if he could find anything that would identify them. As he'd suspected, they weren't carrying anything except a little money, some tobacco, and extra shells for their guns. He stowed their

24

belongings away in their saddlebags, finished the burying, and then rode west again, this time leading the two extra horses.

Luck was the only thing that had saved him, he knew. If he hadn't stopped to take that nap, the two men would have picked up his trail again and probably bushwhacked him sooner or later. He had accidentally crossed them up by stopping when he did, though.

Well, he wasn't going to complain about a little luck. It had saved his hide before and probably would again. A man needed all the breaks he could when he was in a line of work that just naturally led folks to go gunning for him every so often.

Longarm grinned, shook his head wearily, lit a cheroot, and kept riding.

Chapter 3

The Federal Building on Colfax Avenue in Denver was an impressive edifice, but Longarm had been working out of the building for so long that he seldom paid any attention to it. He went up the steps to the entrance, through the high-ceilinged lobby, and climbed the stairs to the second floor, where the office of the chief marshal for the Western District was located. Henry was at his desk pounding away on his typewriting machine when Longarm entered the outer office and flipped his hat onto the hat tree next to the door.

"Howdy, Henry," Longarm said to the clerk, who despite his prissy ways had become sort of a friend over the years. "Billy in his office?"

"Marshal Vail was expecting you back yesterday," Henry said without looking up from his typing. He could really make that machine sing, Longarm had thought more than once.

"Ran into a little trouble," Longarm said with a shrug.

That made Henry pause in his typing. "Where's the prisoner?" he asked as he looked up. "Did you leave him at the House of Detention or—oh, Lord, he's not *dead,* is he?"

"Honest, Henry, I never—"

The clerk stood up and glowered at Longarm. "Wouldn't it be possible, *just once,* for you to serve a warrant and bring back a prisoner without killing him and probably shooting up a whole town in the process?"

"Don't pucker your asshole over it, old son," Longarm snapped, losing his patience. "It just so happens I didn't shoot this here prisoner. He was already dead when I got to La Junta. He tried to escape a few days ago, and the local marshal had to shoot him."

"Oh." Henry blinked. "I see. Well, have you written up a report on the matter?"

"Right here." Longarm took the documents out of his coat pocket and laid them on Henry's desk. The stack included the original warrant and transfer papers, the report Longarm had written this morning in his rented room on the other side of Cherry Creek, and the receipts for his expenses in La Junta.

Henry looked through the papers and muttered, "Well, this seems to be in order. You'll still have to talk to Marshal Vail, however."

"I'll fill him in on what happened." Longarm went to the door of the inner office as Henry sat down behind the desk again. He paused and added, "See, I don't always shoot the gents I'm supposed to pick up."

"Yes, well, I suppose I'm sorry for jumping to conclusions."

"All the fellas I shot on *this* trip were just sort of incidental-like." Longarm opened the door, grinned as Henry looked up and gawked, and stepped quickly into Vail's office before the startled clerk could say anything else. He shut the door behind him and turned to face the chief marshal.

Billy Vail had thickened some around the middle, and there was a lot more pink scalp visible on top of his head than there had been a few years earlier. He looked up from the paperwork scattered on his desk and growled, "Sit down, Longarm. I expected you back yesterday."

"A couple of fellas jumped me on the way, and dealing with them slowed me up a mite." Longarm sat down in the red leather chair in front of the desk.

Vail frowned. "Bushwhackers?"

"That's what they had in mind," Longarm said. "As it turned out, we sort of surprised each other before they had a chance to get the drop on me."

"I don't suppose you apprehended them?"

"Now, Billy," Longarm chided, "you know I would have if I could. There wasn't really much time—"

"So you killed them both."

Longarm shrugged.

Vail leaned back in his chair, clasped his hands over his ample belly, and shook his head. "I don't suppose you know *why* they were gunning for you?"

"I figure it was because of that bank robbery back in La Junta that the town marshal and I sort of broke up."

"Bank robbery?" repeated Vail.

"That's right. You recollect a young jasper name of Hobie Carson?"

Vail thought for a second and then nodded, and Longarm quickly filled him in on the violent welcome that had awaited him in La Junta. When he was through, Vail said, "I guess it was a good thing you happened to be there. What about that prisoner you went after? Where's he?"

"Well now, Billy, that's another story. You see, he was dead when I got there."

"Dead!"

Longarm nodded soberly. "It's all in my report. Henry's got it, so I reckon he'll type it up and give it to you later."

"Save me the suspense," Vail snapped. "Tell me about it now."

Longarm did, explaining everything from the unexpected shootout when he rode into La Junta to the discovery of Jack Paige's demise at the hand of Marshal Frank Nemo to the fight with the two men who had been tracking him. When he was finished, Vail sighed and said, "It would sure be nice to send you out on a job where nobody got killed."

"You know me, Billy," Longarm said. "I'm a peaceable man."

Vail just snorted.

Longarm looked at the banjo clock on the wall and saw that the hour was getting along toward midday. "Well, if you don't have anything else for me to do right now, Billy, I reckon I'll go get me some lunch."

"Sit back down," Vail said. "Seeing as you're here and don't have anything better to do right now, I think it'd be a good idea for you to go through some of these reports the Justice Department keeps sending to me. Could be you'll be sitting in this chair one of these days."

"God forbid," Longarm muttered under his breath.

Vail ignored the interruption and pressed on. "And I want you to have a good idea of just what the job of chief marshal entails. Here." He shoved a stack of papers across the desk toward Longarm. "Take these, go through 'em, and write a report that summarizes their conclusions."

Longarm frowned darkly at the pile of documents. "I swear, Billy, you're starting to sound like some kind of schoolma'am. You know how I feel about paperwork."

"Somebody's got to do it," Vail said blandly.

Longarm sighed. He didn't look on this chore as punishment really, since he knew Billy couldn't blame him for Jack Paige being dead, but he still felt a little resentful. Still, Vail had been a pretty good boss, as bosses went, and Longarm didn't want to wrangle with him too much.

"All right," he said heavily. "I'll do it, Billy."

"There's an empty office down the hall. Have Henry show you the one."

Longarm nodded, stood up, and picked up the papers from Vail's desk. Feeling worse than if he'd been heading into a den of rattlers, Longarm trudged out of the chief marshal's office.

Henry smiled at the stack of documents in Longarm's arms as the rangy deputy paused by his desk. "You mean Marshal Vail's actually got you doing paperwork?" he asked in mock astonishment.

"Don't push it," Longarm warned, his eyes narrowed down to slits. "Just show me where I can work on this . . . this . . ." For one of the few times in his life, he was at a loss for words.

Still grinning, Henry led Longarm down the hall, and Longarm wondered just how much trouble he could get into for choking a goddamned smug little asshole of a clerk.

The reports had to do with the different types of crimes being committed most often in the Western states that were the bailiwick of Billy Vail's office, and they were actually more interesting than Longarm had expected. He had long since concluded that folks were capable of just about any kind of lawbreaking, but he ran across a few items in the paperwork that made even him raise his eyebrows. By the time his stomach reminded him that he hadn't eaten lunch, it was already well after noontime.

He left the papers spread out on the desk in the office where he had been working, put his hat on, and walked quietly down the hall, figuring to slip past Vail's office without Henry noticing him. He reached the stairs successfully and went down them with a grin on his face, feeling like a little boy who had just successfully escaped from a strict parent. Maybe the chore hadn't turned out to be as bad as he'd expected, but he still chafed at being shut up inside on a pretty day.

Longarm put an unlit cheroot between his teeth and sauntered down the street, nodding to the ladies he passed and enjoying the late summer sunshine. He planned to have lunch at a nearby restaurant run by a Chinaman who could hold his own with any chuck wagon cook on the range.

There was a sudden patter of footsteps nearby, the sound telling him that whoever was coming up the sidewalk behind him was female. The steps were too light and quick to belong to a man. Longarm stopped and turned around. Sure enough, he caught a glimpse of green eyes, red hair under a bottle-green hat, and fair skin dusted lightly with freckles, just before the young woman collided with his chest and gave an unladylike grunt of surprise.

"Hold on there," Longarm said as he put a hand on her arm to steady her. "A little lady like you is liable to hurt herself running along a crowded sidewalk like that."

Her eyes flashed green fire as she looked up at him and said, "I am *not* a little lady, as you put it, sir. I am a fully grown woman."

Without being too obvious about it, Longarm had already taken in the elegant curves of the body being hugged by the dark green dress the redhead wore. He nodded and said, "Yes, ma'am, I can see that. Sorry I got in your way."

"You weren't in my way," she snapped back at him. "I was trying to catch up with you. You *are* Deputy Marshal Long, aren't you?"

Longarm frowned in puzzlement as he nodded. As far as he could remember, he had never seen this young woman before, and he was pretty sure he would recollect it if he had. She was lovely, with a charm that was both innocent and sensuous at the same time.

He touched a finger to the brim of his hat and said, "That's right. I'm sorry, ma'am, but I don't reckon we've been introduced."

"My name is Maureen Paige. And we've already established that you're Deputy Long."

Longarm's frown deepened. "Paige, did you say?"

"That's right. I'm married . . . I *was* married . . . to Jack Paige. I believe you know the name."

Longarm's muscles tensed. It was damned hard at the best of times to predict what a female was going to do, and now that he was confronted with the grieving widow of the prisoner he'd been supposed to pick up at La Junta, he had no idea what to expect. It was possible that Maureen Paige might blame *him* for what had happened to her husband.

Only she didn't really look like she was overcome with grief, Longarm decided. Her expression was solemn, right enough, but her emotions were definitely under control. He figured it was unlikely she would pull a pistol from her purse and start blazing away at him.

He reached up and took his hat off, saying, "I'm sorry, ma'am. I didn't know Jack Paige was married, and I sure never expected to run into his widow here in Denver. The paperwork I saw didn't say anything—"

"I know," she broke in. "You see, Deputy Long, I'm from Pennsylvania. That's where I met Jack and married him. And that's where he left me when he came west."

Longarm recalled the charges from the warrant. Jack Paige had been some sort of swindler who'd hatched an elaborate scheme to sell the same water rights over and over. At least that was what he had been charged with. Longarm didn't really have anything to do with determining the man's guilt or innocence. That was a chore for a judge and jury at a trial, of which there wouldn't be one since Jack Paige was now resting, peacefully or not, under six feet of sod in La Junta's potter's field.

Longarm's curiosity was aroused, though, and he asked Maureen Paige, "You mean he abandoned you back there in Pennsylvania?" That was hard for Longarm to believe, because Maureen was mighty attractive, but then he'd never had bunco charges hanging over his head either, so it was hard to say *what* he would do under those circumstances.

Maureen was the kind of woman who might make a man risk jail, though. There were fires smoldering in those green eyes . . .

"Jack claimed he was innocent, Deputy Long. I'm sure you've heard many such claims of innocence. He said he would establish himself out here in the West and then send for me secretly, so that he couldn't be tracked down when I came to join him. It . . ." Her voice faltered slightly. "It's my belief now that he *was* guilty, and I don't think he ever would have sent for me. Perhaps he genuinely intended to when he told me that, but he wouldn't have."

"Well, ma'am, I'm sorry, but I reckon we'll never know, because . . . well . . ."

"I know my husband is dead, Deputy." Maureen's voice was crisp and cool again now, just like her appearance. "My father has friends in the Justice Department in Washington, and he was informed by them that Jack had been captured in a small town in Colorado called La Junta. My father told me, and against his advice I started out here immediately on the train. I knew I could check with the chief marshal's office here in Denver and find out where Jack was being held. Instead, when I arrived a few minutes ago, I was told by a nice young man in Marshal Vail's office that Jack had been killed while in custody. He pointed you out to me as you were leaving the building and said that you could give me the whole story."

Damn that Henry, Longarm cursed to himself. Here he'd thought he had slipped out of the Federal Building without being noticed, and all the time Henry had been siccing this widow on him. Well, there was nothing to do but answer her questions, he supposed. She deserved to hear the truth.

"Yes, ma'am, Mrs. Paige, I can tell you what happened, I reckon. But I promise you right now, I didn't have anything to do with your husband's death." Might as well head off any hard feelings as soon as he could.

"I know," she said, nodding. "The clerk in Marshal Vail's office told me that much. I hope it's all right that I hurried after you."

33

"Sure," Longarm told her. He glanced around at the crowded sidewalk. Pedestrians had been stepping around them as they talked, and crowds had always made Longarm uncomfortable. He went on. "Tell you what. I was on my way to have some lunch. Why don't you come with me, and I'll tell you everything I know about what happened."

Maureen hesitated as she considered his offer, then finally nodded after a moment. "I suppose that would be all right. To tell you the truth, I came straight to the Federal Building from the train station, and I haven't eaten. I'm rather hungry."

"Well, we'll just take care of that." Longarm linked his arm with hers, the gesture a polite one only, and led her down the street toward the Chinaman's place.

Under the circumstances, there wasn't a lot of chatting going on. Maureen Paige might not be bawling her eyes out for her dead husband, but composed or not, she was still a recent widow. Longarm wasn't going to spin the same line of blarney he normally would have when he was going to lunch with a pretty, redheaded young filly. *Just try to act a mite dignified, old son,* he told himself.

Even though the noon rush was over, the Chinaman's was still pretty busy, but the waiters knew Longarm and got him a table without him and Maureen having to wait more than a minute or two. They were ushered to a table with a red-and-white checkered cloth on it, set in a corner where a couple of big potted plants gave a little privacy. Longarm could have told the waiter who brought them there that such seclusion wasn't necessary today—he wasn't trying to make any sort of romantic impression on Maureen after all—but that might have necessitated explaining *why* they had been steered into this corner. Better to just keep his mouth shut about the matter, Longarm decided.

They didn't get down to business until they had studied the menus and given their orders to the waiter. Longarm went with his usual steak and potatoes, while Maureen had baked chicken. Once they were alone, Longarm looked across the table at his companion and said, "You mentioned your father having friends in the Justice Department. Is he anybody I'd know?"

"You might," she said. "He was Assistant Attorney General under President Grant."

Longarm blinked, then shook his head. "Nope, I don't reckon we ever crossed paths. I don't get to Washington City too often."

He didn't mention the well-known fact that just about every politician in Washington during old U.S. Grant's Administration had been as crooked as a Texas sidewinder. Maybe Maureen's father had been one of the few honest ones, and Longarm was willing to give him the benefit of the doubt. Anyway, it didn't really have anything to do with what they were talking about.

"I'm sorry you came all the way out here just to hear bad news," he went on. "I know it's a long, hard trip by train, being bounced around and breathing cinders and smoke. Quicker than it used to be by stagecoach, though."

"The trip wasn't too awfully unpleasant," Maureen said. "I have to admit, however, that I was disturbed when I heard about Jack."

"Well, sure, any woman would be," Longarm said, "hearing that her husband was—"

"No, Deputy Long, you misunderstand me. It's been over a year since Jack left me in Pennsylvania, and I had long since given up hope of him sending for me as he said he would. I wanted to confront him one more time, and see what he had to say for himself. I . . . I suppose I might have held out a small shred of hope . . ." Abruptly, Maureen shook her head. "But there's no point in talking about that now. What disturbed me, and what I want to know more about from you, are the circumstances of his death."

Longarm frowned again. "How much did Henry tell you?"

35

"You mean Marshal Vail's clerk? Only that Jack was killed while in the custody of the town marshal in the settlement where he was captured. Could you tell me the man's name?"

"Nemo," Longarm said. "Frank Nemo."

"Nemo. That's a strange name."

Longarm hadn't thought about it, but he supposed she was right. Something about it struck him as familiar, although he couldn't have said just what it was. He knew, though, that folks could have all sorts of names and that there was no accounting for some of them.

"He seemed to be a pretty good lawman," Longarm said. "Some gents tried to hold up the town bank while I was there, and Marshal Nemo and I had to take 'em to task about it."

"You mean there was a shootout, don't you?"

"Well, I reckon there was," Longarm admitted. "That didn't have anything to do with your husband either. He'd been dead for a couple of days when I got to La Junta."

Maureen didn't say anything. She just sat there looking across the table at him, her gaze calm and intelligent but still somehow unsettling.

"He was killed trying to escape," Longarm went on. "He jumped the marshal and then tried to gun him. Nemo didn't have any choice but to shoot your husband, I'm afraid."

Maureen took the news without flinching. She sat silently for several moments, a slight frown gradually appearing on her face. At last she shook her head and said quietly, "That's impossible."

"What's impossible?" asked Longarm.

"Jack was never a . . . a physically courageous man, Deputy Long. He would never start a fight with a marshal and then try to shoot his way out of jail. It just wouldn't happen that way."

"The threat of going to prison can make a man do things he normally wouldn't," Longarm pointed out.

"Yes, perhaps, but I know Jack. I was married to him for almost two years before he fled those charges. He'd do his

36

best to avoid capture, but once he was a prisoner, he would take his punishment and try to find a way to turn it all to his advantage."

It was Longarm's turn not to say anything as he chewed over what she had told him. Her sincerity was obvious, but just because she believed what she was telling him didn't make it the truth.

Finally, he said, "I reckon Billy Vail might let you read the report I turned in, considering the circumstances, and I got the facts straight from Marshal Nemo. You can see for yourself what happened if you like."

"I'm not sure that's necessary. I believe the report will match up with what you've told me, Deputy. I'm just not sure that you have all the facts."

Longarm's eyes narrowed slightly. "Are you saying that Nemo lied about what happened?"

"He must have."

"There wouldn't be any reason for him to do that."

"What about some sort of reward?" Maureen asked.

Longarm thought back to the state reward dodgers on Paige that Nemo had shown him. The various bounties on the man might have added up to a tidy little sum, but hardly a fortune. And there was one other point that made Maureen's suspicions groundless.

"Your husband wouldn't have been worth a penny more dead than alive," Longarm said as he shook his head. "If Nemo put in for those rewards—and there's no legal reason why he shouldn't have—they'd have been paid just as quick if your husband had been turned over to me. If you're thinking that Nemo pulled something underhanded, I just don't see it."

"Naturally, you'd defend another lawman—"

"No, ma'am," Longarm said sharply, hating to interrupt a lady but not wanting her to get the wrong idea. "I've dealt with more than one jackleg star-packer. Some of 'em are behind bars, and some of 'em are in the ground. My boss accuses me of cutting corners sometimes, but I reckon putting up with crooked lawmen ain't one of my failings."

"I'm sorry, Deputy Long," Maureen murmured. "I didn't mean to imply you were less than honest. I'm just confused. I don't know what to make of this entire matter. And . . . and there's a part of me that remembers when I was happily married to Jack . . ."

Doggone it, Longarm thought. After all this time she was going to puddle up and go to weeping. But then she took a deep breath and got her emotions under control again, and a moment later their food arrived, which kept them busy for a while. By the time the meal was over, Maureen Paige was cool and calm again.

"Thank you for all the information you've given me," she said as they finished their coffee. "You've been very kind."

"Not at all," Longarm said. "Just wish I could've had better news for you. If you don't mind my saying so, Mrs. Paige, I think if I'd been your husband, I wouldn't have run out on you like that, no matter what folks said I'd done. Hope you don't mind a little plain talk."

For the first time since they had met, Maureen smiled, and it made her even prettier. She said, "I have a feeling, Deputy Long, that if you were my husband, you never would have been charged with swindling. Your crimes would have been of a more direct, active nature."

"Thanks . . . I reckon." Longarm stood up and reached for his hat. "You want me to walk you back to the Federal Building and take you up to see Billy Vail?"

Maureen shook her head. "That won't be necessary. I had my bags sent from the station to the Windsor Hotel, and I want to make sure they arrived there as they were supposed to. And I *am* rather tired."

"Sure. I'll walk you over to the Windsor."

"No, thank you. I . . . I'd rather be by myself right now, if you don't mind, Deputy Long."

Longarm's brow furrowed. He didn't much like the idea of Maureen walking around town by herself, but on the other hand nothing was likely to happen to her in broad daylight in the middle of Denver. "All right," he said. "Whatever you think's best."

Again she smiled at him and shook his hand almost like a man. "Thank you, Deputy." She turned and walked out of the restaurant, every inch the lady.

Longarm watched her go, knowing that he would never fully solve all the intricate puzzles of female nature. On the surface, Maureen Paige was reserved, but he sensed there was more to her than that. She was stubborn, yet her emotions were on a tight rein. She acted like she didn't love her husband anymore, yet she had jumped on a train and come on a long cross-country jaunt as soon as she got word of his whereabouts. She was more than Longarm could figure out on first meeting, that was for sure.

But maybe she'd be around Denver for a while, and he'd have a chance to try again. There were a hell of a lot worse ways for a man to spend his time.

Chapter 4

But he didn't see Maureen again during the next few days, and then Billy Vail had a job for him and sent him off up to Wyoming—where he damn near got killed more than once—and when he came back to Denver he didn't happen to run into Maureen either. There were warrants to be served down at Pueblo, so Vail handed him that assignment next. When Longarm got back after that trip, he checked at the Windsor Hotel and was told that Mrs. Maureen Paige had left two weeks earlier. Cussing his bad luck, Longarm went about his business, and almost before he knew it, a month had passed since his trip to La Junta to pick up Jack Paige.

Autumn was in full swing now, the days crisp and the air so clear the Front Range looked to be right outside the city limits, the nights often downright cold. Longarm had been in town for over a week and was getting a little antsy one morning as he strolled into Billy Vail's office, only half an hour after the time he was supposed to report for work.

"The marshal is waiting for you," Henry said sharply, a tone of rebuke in his voice. Longarm could tell that Billy had been doing some snarling and growling, just like an old dog, and Henry had undoubtedly been the target of the grousing.

"Well, I'm here," Longarm said calmly around the cheroot in his mouth. "I'll go in and see about cooling off the old bear."

Henry cleared his throat meaningfully and cut his eyes over, looking at something behind Longarm. The rangy deputy turned slowly and hung his hat on the tree, using that as an excuse to see what Henry was trying to warn him about. A woman sat there on the cracked leather divan beside the door. She gave Longarm a disapproving look. He couldn't place her, but she looked familiar to him somehow.

"Marshal Vail said both of you were to go in as soon as you got here," Henry said.

Longarm smiled at the woman and said, "Reckon this little fella means you're supposed to see Marshal Vail with me, ma'am." He offered her his arm, more out of habit than anything else.

The woman stood up but didn't take his arm. "I know exactly what he means, Deputy," she said coolly. "And now that you've kept us all waiting this long, I don't want to waste any more time. Come along."

"Yes, ma'am," muttered Longarm as he followed her toward the door of Vail's office.

She was about thirty-five years old, he figured, with short, feathery blond hair. She wore a gray hat and a dark brown tweed suit that showed off a figure which wasn't saloon-girl slim but wasn't too bad either. Her bust was rather small, but following her the way he was, Longarm had a good view of an impressively firm rear end.

He took his gaze off her rump as he went into Billy Vail's office with her and heard the chief marshal say, "There you are at last, Longarm! Sit down, Mrs. Dunston, and I hope you'll pardon the delay."

"All part of the job, Marshal," the woman said as she took the red leather chair without waiting for Longarm to hold it for her. She had a crisp, efficient air about her, as

41

if she wasn't accustomed to waiting for niceties from any man.

Longarm pulled over one of the straight chairs and sat down, crossing his legs as he wondered what the hell this was all about.

Vail started by saying, "I'm not sure if you two know each other. Mrs. Dunston, this is Deputy Marshal Custis Long. Longarm, let me introduce Mrs. Harriet Dunston."

"Pleased to meet you, ma'am," Longarm said with a nod to the woman.

"I've heard of you, Deputy Long," Harriet Dunston replied. "You're quite famous in the House of Detention. There are a great many stories about the marshal called Longarm."

His teeth clenched a little tighter on his cheroot as he repeated, "House of Detention?"

"Mrs. Dunston's a matron there," Vail supplied. He rattled some papers on his desk. "The two of you are going to be working together."

Longarm looked at his boss. "Is that so?"

"Do you object?" Harriet asked immediately.

"Didn't say that," Longarm replied with a shake of his head. "This is just the first I've heard of it."

Vail said, "I received word this morning that a woman named Ellen Haley has been arrested in the town of Macready, over in the foothills of the Front Range near Loveland."

Longarm nodded. "Been there a time or two."

"This Haley woman has a federal warrant out on her for passing counterfeit stock certificates. You and Mrs. Dunston are going to go over there and pick her up."

"Reckon I could handle that job by myself, Billy," Longarm said mildly.

Harriet didn't give Vail a chance to answer. She said, "I'm sure you could, Deputy, but regulations require that a matron be present any time a female prisoner is being transported from one facility to another."

"Ain't like I never brought in a female prisoner by myself," Longarm muttered.

"There were extenuating circumstances in those cases," Vail pointed out, "like you were alone when you captured 'em. This is different, and there's no good reason not to follow regulations in this case."

Longarm shrugged. "You're the boss, Billy."

That was true enough, but Longarm didn't have to like the assignment. Not that he had anything against Harriet Dunston. She was a mite sharp-tongued, sure, but he had never had anything against females who spoke their own minds. It was just that he was used to working by himself.

"There's no spur line over to Macready, so you'll have to travel by buggy," Vail said as he pushed documents across the desk. "Here's the warrant and transfer papers."

Harriet picked up the documents before Longarm could reach for them and tucked them into her purse, which brought a frown to Longarm's face. He didn't say anything as Billy flashed him a warning look.

"I can handle a buggy," Harriet said.

"I'll draw a saddle horse and ride." Longarm sat back and waited for Vail to object, but the chief marshal just nodded

"That's what I figured. It'll take you a couple of days to get there, so the sooner you get started, the better."

Harriet stood up. "I'll pack my things and be ready to leave in a half hour, Deputy Long."

Longarm nodded as he stood up and said, "Fine by me. So long, Billy."

He held the door open for Harriet as they went out of the office. Since they were both leaving the building, it was natural enough for them to walk side by side down the corridor, although Longarm slowed his pace a little so that he wouldn't outdistance her as they went down the stairs to the lobby.

Harriet paused at the top of the steps outside that led down to Colfax Avenue. "Shall we meet back here, Deputy Long?"

43

"Reckon that'd be all right. And my friends call me Longarm."

A hint of a smile played around her mouth. "I wasn't sure you wanted to be friends. We can keep this strictly on a coworker basis if you'd like."

"Well, I reckon that depends on how your husband feels about you traveling halfway across the state with another fella."

Harriet shook her head. "Oh, I'm not married. I've been a widow for the past eight years."

"Sorry," Longarm said.

"That's all right. I get a great deal of satisfaction out of my work."

"At the House of Detention? I thought you looked a mite familiar, so I suppose I've seen you there a time or two in the past."

"No doubt. Well, we'd better get busy, hadn't we, Longarm?"

"Yes, ma'am, I reckon so." He touched a finger to the brim of his hat. "See you in half an hour."

They went their separate ways, a grin tugging at Longarm's mouth as he strode down the street toward his rented room. Harriet Dunston seemed to be all business, and that was fine if that was the way she wanted it. Besides, on the way back they'd have that prisoner along. Longarm didn't really expect any friskiness on Harriet's part during the trip.

But a man could never tell for sure, which was one of the joys of life as far as Longarm was concerned.

If Longarm had thought he detected a hint of something other than pure devotion to duty in Harriet Dunston, by the time they reached the settlement of Macready, he was sure he had been wrong. Harriet wasn't mean or argumentative, but she never got much above the level of strict civility either. He had seen her smile maybe three times, and during the long miles of riding beside the buggy as she drove toward the foothills of the Front Range, their small talk had garnered the

44

information that her late husband had been a Denver police-man before he was killed in a robbery he had the misfortune to interrupt, and that she had a daughter in her teens who was in a girls' school in Kansas City. Longarm thought that was more than she could have afforded on a matron's salary from the House of Detention, but Harriet explained that the owner of the store where her husband had foiled the robbery had given her a sizable cash settlement in gratitude after her husband's death.

Money always came in handy, Longarm supposed, but it didn't replace somebody to hold you during the night. Harriet seemed to be coping just fine, though, so he kept his comments to himself.

They spent one night on the trail, Harriet sleeping in a small tent she had packed into the back of the buggy, Longarm rolling his blankets under a tree. Then, late in the afternoon of the second day, they reached Macready, which Longarm remembered as a brawling, mining camp sort of town. The place had settled down considerably, he saw as he and Harriet went down the main street. The buildings were all permanent now, the tents and plank-and-tarpaper shacks long gone. The street wasn't paved and there weren't any gas lamps on the sidewalks, like back in Denver, but Macready was definitely getting civilized.

Longarm spotted a sign saying MARSHAL'S OFFICE hanging over the boardwalk in front of a red-brick building and pointed it out to Harriet. She swung the buggy over to the hitch rack in front of the office. Longarm dismounted, tied the reins of his horse to the post, then wrapped the reins of the buggy horse around the rack as well. He would have helped Harriet down from the buggy, but she was already standing beside him before he was finished with the horses.

They stepped up onto the boardwalk, and Longarm held the door open for her. As she entered, she said, "Excuse me, Marshal, but I'm Harriet Dunston from the Denver Federal

House of Detention, and this is Deputy Marshal Long—"

"Howdy, Custis!"

Longarm came to a startled halt beside Harriet and saw Frank Nemo putting a rifle back into a rack behind the desk on the other side of the room. He was dressed much the same as he had been in La Junta, and there was still a badge on his vest. This one was a little different in design, however.

Nemo strode across the room and extended a hand to Longarm. "Well, who'd've thought it'd be you they'd send out to pick up this prisoner? Just like back in La Junta, eh, but without the bank robbery this time, I hope."

"You're the marshal here in Macready now, Frank?" asked Longarm.

"That's right. Been on the job about a week. Got tired of that flatland over by Kansas and decided to come see some mountains again. I was lucky enough to find a place that needed an experienced lawman, so here I am."

Harriet put in, "I'm glad you two know each other, but we have a prisoner to pick up, Marshal."

Nemo's smile disappeared and was replaced by a solemn frown. "Well, now, there's a story goes along with that," he began.

Longarm suddenly felt a shiver go up his back. "When you said this was just like back in La Junta, you didn't mean the prisoner we're after is dead, did you?"

"I'm afraid so, Custis."

"Son of a bitch!" Longarm blurted out, forgetting for a second that Harriet was standing beside him. Of course, she'd likely heard a lot worse in the House of Detention back there in Denver. "What happened?"

Nemo rolled up his left sleeve to show a thick bandage wrapped around his forearm. "The lady wasn't much of a lady. She had a knife hidden somewhere on her—don't ask me where, because I sure don't know—and she tried to carve me from gizzard to gullet yesterday. I got my arm up just in time, but she still cut me right down to the bone. The doc here sewed it up for me."

"But what about Miss Haley?" demanded Harriet.

Longarm said, "You didn't . . ."

"I didn't gun her, if that's what you mean." Nemo sounded a bit quarrelsome now, as if he resented the questions. "I gave her a good hard shove to get her away from me with that blade, and she tripped and fell. Hit her head on the corner of that stove over there." He pointed to a heavy, black cast-iron stove on the other side of the gun rack. "Doc said she stove in her skull when she hit it. It was just an accident, Custis."

"This is outrageous," Harriet said hotly. "We come here to pick up a federal prisoner, and now you tell us she's dead!"

"Accidents happen, ma'am," Nemo said. His tone was curt, and Longarm sensed they were on the brink of trouble.

He said, "Hold on now. There's no need to go to arguing about this. What'd you do with the body, Frank?"

"She was buried earlier today, at county expense. Right after the coroner's inquest, in fact. Which resulted in a verdict of accidental death while in legal custody, by the way. You're welcome to talk to the coroner."

Longarm shook his head. "Don't reckon that's necessary But you got to admit, it's a mite strange, Frank, the way this worked out after what happened last time."

Harriet shot a sharp glance at him. "Last time? What was that about some place called La Junta?"

"I lost another prisoner Custis was supposed to pick up a while back," Nemo told her. "That fella tried to escape, just like Miss Haley did. I admit it's a coincidence, but you've been a lawman for a long time, Custis. You've had a prisoner or two make a break for the tall and uncut, haven't you?"

Longarm shrugged. "It happens, all right. But usually the gents who've tried to kill me were facing worse charges than passing phony stock certificates."

"No accounting for what a criminal will do. You know that."

"Well, I can tell you, Marshal Nemo, I intend to make a full report on this matter," said Harriet. "Marshal Vail in Denver may want to look into it himself."

Nemo spread his hands. "Fine by me. I don't have anything to hide."

Harriet looked like she was ready to chew nails in frustration. "Come on," Longarm said to her as he put a hand lightly on her arm. "This late in the day there's no point in starting back to Denver. We might as well get us a couple of hotel rooms."

She nodded. "You're right, I suppose." To Nemo, she added, "My apologies if I sounded suspicious, Marshal. But I take my job seriously, and if I don't come back with the prisoner I went after, I expect to have a good reason."

Longarm thought she had the best reason of all—Ellen Haley was dead. But he gently steered Harriet out of the office without saying anything else, glancing back at Nemo as they reached the doorway. The local lawman shrugged apologetically and once again spread his hands as if to ask Longarm what else he could have done.

Not having been there, Longarm couldn't answer that question. But he had to admit that the coincidence of Frank Nemo being forced to kill another escaping prisoner bothered him some. It was stretching things already to run into Nemo here in Macready when a month earlier the man had been the marshal in La Junta, nearly clear across the state. Longarm was willing to accept that; small-town badge-toters like Nemo tended to drift from place to place, sometimes on just such a whim as Nemo had mentioned. Another reason lawmen drifted was that small-town people just got tired of having a fast gun around even if the fast gun belonged to the law. The story of Ellen Haley's death was a little harder to swallow.

Yet he had no proof that Nemo was lying about it, or even any reason to think that the marshal might not have been telling the truth. Like Nemo said, prisoners sometimes tried to escape, and when they did, they sometimes wound up dead. It was just a fact of life when you were a lawman.

Still, Longarm wished that the area between his shoulder blades didn't feel quite so itchy when he turned his back on Frank Nemo.

Macready had a fine brick hotel now, complete with dining room, and Longarm and Harriet Dunston ate their supper there after checking in. They took separate rooms, of course, and Longarm told himself not to be disappointed when the rooms weren't even adjoining.

While they were eating, Harriet asked him flat out, "Do you believe Marshal Nemo's story, Longarm?"

"No reason not to believe it." He told her about Maureen Paige's visit to Denver and the young woman's insistence that her husband wouldn't have tried to escape from Nemo's custody in La Junta, and certainly wouldn't have attempted to shoot it out with the lawman. He explained his reasoning why Maureen had to be wrong, then concluded by saying, "The same thing holds true here. Nemo didn't have anything to gain by killing Ellen Haley. And if she didn't try to carve him up with a knife, he wouldn't have told us that story and showed us the bandage on his arm. He knows we can find out if he's telling the truth just by asking the sawbones who sewed him up."

Harriet nodded slowly. "That makes sense, all right. But I just have the strangest feeling about the whole thing."

Longarm took a sip of his coffee and then said, "Well, to tell you the truth, Harriet, so do I. But without any more to go on than a hunch, I don't reckon there's much we can do about it."

She looked intently across the table at him, studying him for a moment before saying, "Somehow, I also have the feeling that you've acted on nothing more than a hunch in the past."

"Maybe so. But when I did, it was a *strong* hunch."

49

"I still intend to make a full report to Marshal Vail on the matter."

"So do I," said Longarm. "Seems like that's half of a lawman's job, filling out forms and writing up reports."

They dropped the subject of Frank Nemo and Ellen Haley and filled the rest of the meal with small talk. When they were finished, Harriet said good night and went up to her room, while Longarm wandered into the hotel's barroom to smoke a couple of cheroots, savor a few drinks of Maryland rye, and lose ten bucks in a friendly poker game. Feeling only vaguely frustrated, he went up the stairs and along the second-floor corridor to his room a little before midnight. He and Harriet had agreed to start back to Denver first thing in the morning, so he intended to get a good night's sleep.

Earlier in the evening, he had dropped off his saddle and gear in the room after stabling the horses and the buggy. When he left, he had not only locked the door but wedged a match between the door and the jamb, low down where it wouldn't likely be noticed. It was an old trick but one that generally worked. In the light coming from a lamp at the other end of the hall, Longarm saw the stub of matchstick still in place. No one had entered the room while he was gone, at least not by the door.

He unlocked the room and went inside, still being careful. After pulling the shade on the window and lighting the lamp on a small table, he started undressing. He was down to his long underwear when a soft knock sounded on the door.

Out of habit, Longarm reached for the .44 in the holster he had hung over the nearest bedpost. He snagged the butt of the gun and took it with him as he went over to the door. "Ummm?" he grunted, standing to one side of the panel, knowing that such a response was hard to pinpoint if anybody intended to blow a hole through the door—and him.

"Longarm?"

It was Harriet's voice. Longarm said, "Hold on a minute," and went back to the bed. He holstered the Colt and pulled his pants back on, leaving his shirt off. He was still wearing the long underwear, so he figured he was decent enough.

When he opened the door, Harriet was standing there in a bright green silk dressing gown that was a lot fancier than he would have expected from her. He hadn't seen what she was wearing the night before, since she had gone into the tent still fully dressed. Her hair looked a little fluffier tonight too. Little things, but they made quite a difference.

"Something wrong?" he asked, not quite knowing what response to hope for from her.

"I was just thinking about Marshal Nemo and that prisoner," she replied, dashing Longarm's hopes for the moment. "I thought perhaps we could talk about it some more."

"Sure," Longarm said, moving aside so that she could come in and then shutting the door behind her. "I don't know what else there is to say, though."

"You could be right." She sat down on the bed. "You don't mind me sitting here, do you?"

"Have at it," he said.

"Come sit beside me."

That was a mite unexpected, but Longarm didn't waste any time arguing with her. When he sat down beside her, she went on. "I know that I sometimes take my job too seriously. With my daughter back in Kansas City, though, I . . . I don't really have anything to devote my energies to except my work."

"Nothing wrong with caring about your job," Longarm told her.

"No, but sometimes I get carried away, and I spend all my time thinking about work and ignore the things I should be thinking about."

"Like what?"

"Well . . . like this." She turned on the bed and lifted her arms, putting them around his neck and pulling his head down

51

to kiss him. Her mouth opened, wet and hot and wanting, as she leaned against him. Longarm returned the kiss, letting his tongue slide around hers. When Harriet finally broke the kiss, she said huskily, "There. That's what I should have been thinking about."

"Seems to me like you must've been, at least a little bit," Longarm murmured. He brought his hand up and slid one side of the silk dressing gown back, exposing a small, round, firm breast with an erect, dark red nipple. He bent his head to suck the little bud of urgent flesh into his mouth.

Harriet twined her fingers in his hair and tightened them as he sucked and licked her nipple. Her breathing came more rapidly. Longarm spread the dressing gown and moved his mouth to the other breast. Harriet sank back on the bed, pulling him with her. Her fingers flew to the buttons of his pants and began unfastening them.

When she had the buttons undone, she pushed his pants down past his hips and caressed him through the underwear. "My God!" she gasped, and he didn't know if she was responding to what he was doing to her breasts or to the length and heft of him that she could feel through the material. Didn't much care which it was either. He found the cord that tied the gown around her waist and tugged the knot loose.

Not surprisingly, she wore nothing beneath the gown. Longarm moved his hand down her body, over the gently rounded belly and between the thighs she had spread in invitation to his touch. His fingertips trailed through the fine-spun mesh of blond hair as silky as the gown she still partially wore, and then she gasped again as he reached the wet core of her.

"Oh, Lord, Longarm!" she moaned. "Get those things off and do it to me!"

"Not yet," he told her, and she let out a cry as if he was torturing her.

It had probably been a long time for her and Longarm wanted this to be special. He slid off the bed and went to his knees beside it, his strong hands gripping her soft thighs and spreading them even farther apart as he positioned her. His head moved forward, and he started using his lips and tongue on her, licking, nibbling, probing until her breath rasped wildly in her throat as she panted with desire. He was hard as a damned statue by now and aching to plunge into her, but he held off for as long as he could stand it, tormenting her sweetly.

Finally, in a hoarse voice, Harriet said, "Goddam you, Longarm, you'd better do me *now*!"

He obliged.

He stood up, peeling out of the underwear and kicking it away, and drove into her with such force that both of them skidded part of the way across the bed. Harriet locked her arms around his neck and her legs around his hips as he bucked against her. Her tongue surged into his mouth again as she moaned against his lips.

After a minute she tore her mouth away from his and let her head thrash from side to side as she gulped down air. "More," she panted. "Oh, God, fill me up! Yes, yes . . ."

Longarm was getting a mite carried away himself. He was hitting bottom with each stroke, and when he felt his climax boiling up, he stiffened at the end of a thrust and stayed where he was, buried deep within her. Harriet stifled the scream of her own spasms with the pillow as his seed spilled hotly and wetly into her.

Shuddering, Longarm emptied himself in her, then lay there trying to catch his breath. He eased himself off to the side after a moment and pulled Harriet closer to him, snuggling her in his embrace.

"That . . . that was so *good*," she whispered.

Longarm nodded in agreement, still too winded to talk. What they had just done beat all hell out of worrying about itinerant marshals and prisoners that wound up dead.

After a few minutes, Harriet said quietly, "Thank you, Longarm."

He was able to talk now. "Reckon it's me ought to be thanking you."

"No. You were right, it had been a long time. Much too long. Not since my husband died, in fact."

He frowned. Harriet had been a young, vital woman when her husband was killed. Hell, she was still young and vital as far as he was concerned. He could understand mourning, but to give up loving entirely . . . well, that was just like giving up living.

"I'm glad I was here," he said. "I don't want you thinking I was taking advantage—"

"Oh, no, I don't! I wanted this as much as you. *More* than you. And you were so sweet . . . well, I just think I ought to reciprocate . . ."

With that, she slid out of his embrace and down his body, and her warm lips closed around his still-half-erect shaft.

Longarm caught his breath. "Don't know that that's going to do much good this soon," he began, then stopped abruptly as he realized he was wrong.

Her busy little tongue was doing a hell of a lot of good. And when he was ready again, she rolled over on her hands and knees and stuck that pretty rump of hers up in the air. "This way," she pleaded. "Do it to me this way."

Longarm had never been one to make a lady beg.

They might not be taking a prisoner back to Denver, he thought as he gripped the softness of her hips and slid his length into her again, but he was still damned glad Billy Vail had sent him on this trip!

Chapter 5

Once again Longarm and Harriet Dunston spent one night on the trail during the trip back to Denver, but this time they shared the tent Harriet had brought along. On the surface, Harriet was still the prim and serious matron from the House of Detention, but Longarm knew better. She was a pure-dee wildcat when it came to lovemaking. He figured her imagination had been working overtime during those long years of frustration and denial following her husband's death, and she was eager to try out just about every kind of coupling that anybody could think of. And Harriet could think of a lot of ways!

So Longarm was tired when he returned to Denver after two nights of not much sleep and long days on the trail. It was a satisfying weariness made even better when Harriet kissed him good-bye with a smile on her face that told him she had returned fully to the land of the living. Not that he wanted to give himself too much credit for that. He'd just been in the right place at the right time, that was all. He wasn't going to think so highly of himself as to hold his lovemaking accountable for reviving Harriet's flagging spirits, no sir. To do that would be to go against the grain of his natural humility.

But he was still grinning cockily as he strode down the corridor on the second floor of the Federal Building toward Billy Vail's office.

Vail was an old hand at taking his top deputy down a notch, though, and he wasn't happy about what Longarm had to report.

"Another dead prisoner? My God, Longarm, what's this fella Nemo up to?"

Longarm shook his head as he settled back in the red morocco leather chair. "I don't know that he's up to anything, Billy. If you're willing to accept the coincidences, his story holds up."

"I don't much cotton to coincidences," Vail groused. He sighed. "Unfortunately, I know they happen. What's your gut tell you about this?"

Longarm's wide shoulders rose and fell in a shrug. "I'm not sure everything's on the up and up . . . but I'm not sure it *ain't*. Anyway, I'm don't know what we can do about it either way. Nemo's got a couple of coroners' verdicts to back him up."

"Well, I'm going to do some asking around about this Frank Nemo," declared Vail. "Maybe somebody else knows something about him."

"Thought you might want to do that, Billy. If you come up with anything on him, let me know."

"Count on it," Vail grunted.

The puzzle over the activities of Marshal Frank Nemo got shifted into the background a couple of days later, however, as a flurry of lawlessness took the attention of Longarm, Billy Vail, and nearly everybody else in the Denver office. A train was held up in Boulder, the bank in Colorado Springs was robbed, and an express office in Castle Rock was looted. Longarm was kept busy for several weeks helping to track down the owlhoots involved in the various depredations.

No sooner was he finished with those jobs than a fellow he'd arrested in an influence-peddling scheme earlier in the year finally came to trial. It was a complicated case, full of political maneuverings, and Longarm found himself testifying for several days, then sitting around the courthouse for several more days waiting to see if he was going to be recalled to the stand by any of the myriad of lawyers involved in the trial.

By the time the gent was finally convicted—as he should have been right off, as far as Longarm was concerned—fall had advanced to the point that most of the days were cold and cloudy, and there had already been a couple of light snowfalls. Winter would be coming on soon.

Longarm had the collar of his coat turned up against a chilly west wind as he went up the steps of the Federal Building the day after the conclusion of the trial. He stepped inside, grateful to be out of the wind, and was straightening his coat when he almost bumped into a tall young man named Gilfoyle, who also worked as a deputy out of the Denver office. They had worked together a few times in the past, and Gilfoyle greeted him with a friendly grin.

"Howdy, Longarm," the younger deputy said. "I heard about that trial you were mixed up in. Must've been hard, sitting on your butt in a courtroom for over a week."

Longarm returned the grin. "The hardest part was listening to all the damned lawyers speechifying. If there was some way to make those gents talk plain ol' English, it'd sure speed things up."

Gilfoyle shook his head and said, "It'll never happen. They like the sound of their own voices too much."

Longarm got out a couple of cheroots, gave one to Gilfoyle, and lit his own with a foul-smelling lucifer. Gilfoyle tucked away his cigar, promising to smoke it later. Longarm asked, "What've you been up to lately? Ain't seen you around much."

"Oh, I've been out of town serving warrants for Billy. He gave me a whole wad of them to take care of, then had me finish by picking up a prisoner over at Moss City. You know the place?"

"Heard of it," Longarm said. "Up in the hills betwixt Lyons and Jimtown, ain't it?"

Gilfoyle nodded. "That's right. Funny thing, though. When I got there, the prisoner I was supposed to bring back was already dead."

Longarm's teeth clamped down harder on the cheroot in his mouth. "What?" he grated.

"I said the prisoner was already dead. Shot by the local marshal while trying to escape. Surprised me a little, because the gent wasn't what you'd call a desperado. He'd embezzled a whole pile of cash from the bank where he worked over in Nebraska and then headed this way when he lit out."

Deep furrows appeared in Longarm's brow. "Not exactly the sort you'd figure would try to shoot it out with a lawman, eh?"

"That's right." Gilfoyle shrugged. "Reckon you can't ever tell just what a criminal's going to do, though."

That sounded familiar to Longarm, too damned familiar. He asked, "This local badge, you happen to recollect his name?"

"Frank something or other. Sort of an unusual handle, if I remember right. It's all in my report. I just gave it to Henry to type up." Gilfoyle started frowning too. "What's up, Longarm? Why all the questions?"

"Just some mighty curious coincidences," Longarm told the younger deputy. He didn't want to go into his suspicions with Gilfoyle. He slapped the man on the shoulder and said, "Good to see you again, Gilfoyle. I got to go pay a visit to Billy right now, so I'll see you around."

"You bet, Longarm. Take care."

Longarm nodded and strode quickly toward the stairs, not looking back to see if Gilfoyle was watching him curiously, which the younger deputy probably was. He knew he'd acted spooked by what Gilfoyle had told him.

Hell, he *was* spooked. Coincidence was one thing, but this was getting downright strange.

Henry looked a mite agitated as Longarm came into the office. "I was just about to send someone to look for you," the clerk said. "There's something you need to discuss with Marshal Vail."

"Frank Nemo?" Longarm said.

Henry's head bobbed up and down. "I was typing up Deputy Gilfoyle's report a few minutes ago, and the name struck me as familiar, so I looked it up. I pulled your reports out of the files and sent them in to Marshal Vail, along with the one of Gilfoyle's I just finished."

"Reckon I know what Gilfoyle's said without even reading it." Longarm started toward the door of the inner office.

It was jerked open before he got there. A red-faced Billy Vail snapped, "Henry, send somebody after that dadblamed—well, there you are, Longarm! I was just about to—"

"I reckon I've got that part figured out, Billy," Longarm said dryly. "You were about to send somebody to fetch that dadblamed Deputy Custis Long, right?"

"Get in here," Vail said, ignoring the sarcasm. "We've got something important to talk about."

Longarm heeled the door shut behind him as he went into the office. Vail marched to the desk, picked up a sheaf of papers, and turned to thrust them into Longarm's hands. "The one on top is Gilfoyle's report on an assignment he just got back from," Vail said. "Read it first."

"Don't reckon I have to, because I know what it says already." Longarm scanned the typed words anyway to forestall any more yapping from Billy.

Gilfoyle was a good man, and the report was concise and clear. The embezzlement suspect, one Nelson Hightower, had been picked up in Moss City by the local marshal, Frank Nemo, who had recognized Hightower from his description on a federal wanted poster. Nemo was damned observant, Longarm mused. Hightower was the third federal want he had picked up in recent months.

And the third one to die, as well . . .

The report went on to detail how Hightower had grabbed a gun and tried to escape after Nemo had taken him into custody. It was a virtual repeat of the story Nemo had told Longarm about the death of Jack Paige over in La Junta. Gilfoyle, having no reason to doubt Nemo's word, had accepted the story and written it up that way in his report. This was the younger deputy's first encounter with Nemo, so he hadn't been troubled by the coincidences that had Longarm and Billy Vail so worked up.

Longarm tossed the reports back on Vail's desk and said bluntly, "That son of a bitch is a murderer."

"It's starting to look that way," Vail agreed. "Could be none of those prisoners were really trying to escape. Nemo could've just made it look like they were after he'd killed them." Vail slumped into his chair and motioned for Longarm to sit down too.

"Question now is, what do we do about it?" Longarm asked as he sat.

"Nope. The question is, what *can* we do about it?"

Longarm glared at his superior. "We can't just let the bastard get away with it."

"Damn it, there's the matter of proof." Vail brought a fist down on the desk with a thump. "Nemo's a lawman, and his story in each case is a perfectly plausible one. Besides, there's not much doubt that all three of those prisoners were guilty."

"Of crimes that'd've got 'em sent to prison, not hung," Longarm pointed out. "Nemo didn't have any right to execute 'em."

Vail sighed. "You're right, you're right. But there'll be hell to pay if a federal man goes into a town and starts accusing their local lawman of being some sort of crazy killer. Folks just sort of naturally distrust the federal government to start with, and that includes the people who work for it like you and me."

Billy wasn't telling him anything he didn't already know, Longarm thought. Most citizens took a pretty dim view of criminals, and nobody thought anything about stringing up horse thieves or the like. As long as Nemo kept order and made their town a safe place to live, the citizens of Moss City wouldn't really give a damn how he treated the prisoners in his jail.

Truth to tell, Longarm had never had much sympathy for lawbreakers either. But there were ways to deal with them without folks taking the law into their own hands. Jack Paige and Ellen Haley and Nelson Hightower hadn't represented any threat to the population at large. In each case, they had just wanted a place to hide out, somewhere to live with their ill-gotten gains. Longarm didn't figure they deserved even that much.

But they hadn't deserved a grave in some potter's field either.

Longarm took a deep breath. "Damned if you're not right, Billy. But it don't sit right with me just doing nothing about this."

"Me either," Vail admitted "That's why I want you to ride over to Moss City and take a look around, poke under a few rocks. See if you can find out why Nemo left Macready."

"He'll have a reason," Longarm predicted, "a reason that makes good sense when he tells it."

"You're probably right. But try anyway."

Longarm stood up. "Thanks, Billy. When I remember how I stood there and let Nemo spin those yarns and swallowed 'em whole, I feel like a damned fool. And I don't like that feeling."

"Neither do I." Vail stood up and shook Longarm's hand. "Good luck. You'll need it if you're going to do any good."

Longarm nodded grimly and left the office, pausing in the outer office to check the big map on the wall behind Henry's desk and make sure of the best trail to Moss City. It was north of Macready and deeper in the foothills, another mining community, although there were also several ranches located in the area, Longarm recalled. The last time he'd been there, there hadn't been any law, which meant the place must be growing and settling down some if the citizens had hired themselves a marshal.

He just wished they had picked somebody besides Frank Nemo.

That name nagged at Longarm's brain as he left the Federal Building and headed back to his room to pack for the trip to Moss City. Ever since the first time he had heard it, it had sounded familiar to him, but he had never figured out where he'd heard it before. And as busy as he'd been the past couple of months, he hadn't had much time to devote to thinking about the subject either.

Now all of his concentration was on the unusual name, and as he strode past the Denver Public Library, something suddenly clicked in his brain. Without hesitation, he turned and went up the steps to the entrance of the building.

Longarm didn't particularly want his fellow deputies knowing about it, since they might consider it sort of sissified, but he enjoyed the library. He paid it several visits each month, admittedly when it was close to payday and his money had run so low that other pleasurable pursuits were harder to come by. But he liked the hushed atmosphere when he stepped into the library, so different from the hustle and bustle of the Denver streets outside. He liked the dimness and the dark wood and the shelves and shelves of books that filled up the place. He liked the smell of leather and vellum.

He walked past the counter where the clerks worked and plunged into the maze of shelves. He thought he knew right where to find the book he was looking for, but it wasn't there. A few weeks had passed since he had been in the library, and a quick look around told him that the books had been rearranged in that time. Muttering questions under his breath about why they couldn't leave the blamed things where he could find them, he went back to the counter.

"Pardon me, ma'am," Longarm said to the young woman working there. "Could you tell me where the books by Monsewer Jules Verne have got off to?"

"Jules Verne? Of course." The clerk smiled at him. She was blond, about twenty-five, and nice-looking, with hair piled in a bun and spectacles perched on the end of a cute nose. She wore a frilly white blouse with puffed sleeves, and her bosom filled out the garment just fine. As she got down from the stool she was sitting on, came out from behind the counter, and led Longarm deeper into the maze of shelves, he saw that she had a tall, willowy figure and a damned nice rear end in a long black skirt. He almost felt a pang of regret when she paused in front of a set of shelves and said, "Here are the books you're looking for."

"Thank you kindly." Longarm nodded.

"If you need anything else, don't hesitate to ask," she told him. "My name is Mary Alice."

"Thank you, Mary Alice. I'll sure do that."

She smiled at him and walked back toward the front of the library. Longarm grinned and decided he was going to have to start coming here more often. Then, getting back to the chore that had brought him here, he began scanning the titles on the leather-bound spines of the books in front of him. After a moment, he grunted in satisfaction as he found the one he wanted and took down the thick volume.

As he flipped open the pages, Longarm paused at the title: *20,000 Leagues Under the Sea.* It had been several years since he had read the book, but as he turned to the first page and muttered, "Part One, Chapter One, 'A Shifting Reef,'" the memories came back to him. It was one hell of a yarn, all about how some French scientist called Professor Arronax and his servant Conseil and this Canadian harpooner named Ned Land ran across a mysterious gent who had built himself a submersible boat called a submarine. The whole thing was pretty farfetched but not impossible, Longarm recalled, and anyway it was just a story. The thing Longarm was interested in now was the name of the fella who'd built the submarine.

Seemed he called himself Captain Nemo, and according to the book "Nemo" meant "nothing."

It didn't have any real bearing on the case, but Longarm had to figure that the drifting badge who called himself Frank Nemo had read this book by Monsewer Jules Verne too. Cute, damned cute, he thought. It would have been hard to find a more blatant phony name, and Longarm could have kicked himself for not tumbling to it before now.

He turned to the back of the book and skimmed the last few pages, recalling the excitement he had felt as the *Nautilus,* the mad Captain Nemo's submarine, had been sucked down by the maelstrom, a gigantic whirlpool off the coast of Norway. Professor Arronax and Conseil and Ned Land had escaped from the vessel as it plunged underneath the waves for what could have been the last time. As for the fate of Captain Nemo himself, Verne had left that up in the air. The ending of the story hadn't really been written yet.

And the same was true of Marshal Frank Nemo, but when *this* yarn reached its climax, Longarm intended to be there.

Chapter 6

Finding his way back to the front of the library was such a chore that it put Longarm in mind of a story he'd read once about some ancient king who kept a monster with the head of a bull in a place called the Labyrinth. A man could get turned around pretty easily in this labyrinth of bookshelves, and Longarm halfway expected to see ol' Theseus and the Minotaur go ambling by. Which got him to wondering if the Minotaur had the head of a longhorn or some other breed of bull, and if Theseus had ever thought about bulldoggin' the son of a bitch while they were wrestling around. With all that in his head, it was no wonder he clean forgot to say so long to sweet Mary Alice when he finally found his way out of the place.

Too damn much reading cluttered up a man's mind, Longarm decided.

Packing didn't take long once he reached his room. He put some extra clothes, a supply of cheroots, a mostly full bottle of Maryland rye, two boxes of .44–40 shells, small bags of flour and sugar and salt, and some jerky and dried apples in his saddlebags. He checked his Winchester, put it back in the boot, and hoisted saddle, saddlebags, and all to his shoulder and walked down the street to the remount yard. The hostler gave him a strong-looking claybank gelding. Longarm saddled the horse himself, rather than trusting the chore to the other man. He had a long ride in front of him, and he wanted both himself and the claybank to be comfortable.

It would take about two and a half days to reach Moss City, he figured. As he rode out of Denver, he wondered if the settlement had been named for somebody called Moss, or if it was a reference to the stuff that was supposed to grow on the north side of trees but didn't always. Maybe when he got there he'd ask somebody.

It was more important to figure out what to do about Frank Nemo.

A day's ride, a night's camp, and most of the next day spent in the saddle hadn't given Longarm any answers when he slowed his pace to look for a good spot to spend his second night on the trail. If he pushed on, he might make one of the smaller settlements in the area and find a boardinghouse or at least a livery barn where he could spend the night, but the claybank was tired and so was he. The weather the day before had been overcast and blustery, but today the sky was almost clear and the sunshine held enough warmth to remind him of the summer just past. If conditions stayed that way for a while longer, there was no reason why he couldn't camp out again.

He found a nice little bench on the side of a hill about two hundred yards above the road. A row of pine trees ran along the edge of the bench, screening it off somewhat from anybody passing along the trail. Longarm stumbled on it only because he was looking for a good campsite, and he knew as soon as he saw the place that he had found one. There was grass for the horse and a little spring that bubbled out of the rocks at the base of the bluff on the back side of the bench. The spring pooled up, then meandered off and disappeared back into the bluff. Longarm nodded approvingly and decided he would lay his bedroll beside that pool of crystal-clear water.

After hobbling the horse so that it wouldn't wander too far, Longarm built a small fire and cooked some biscuits to go with the jerky and apples from his saddlebags. He washed down the food with a couple of swallows of Tom Moore, then, as night settled down over the foothills, used a burning twig from the fire to light a cheroot. As he puffed on the cylinder of tobacco, he lifted his eyes away from the blaze and peered off into the gathering shadows. Flames could be hypnotic at night, drawing too much of a man's attention. Besides, staring into a fire ruined whatever night vision a gent had and left him blinded and helpless if he had to suddenly deal with a threat out of the dark.

Longarm knew better than that, and that was why he was able to see the flicker of movement at the edge of the bench. Something was over there in the trees, he thought. Without showing any reaction, he continued puffing on the cheroot and waited for whatever it was to move again.

He considered and then discarded the idea that what he'd seen had been an animal of some kind. His fire had died down somewhat, but it was still blazing brightly enough to alert any animal that man was nearby. Nope, whoever was over there in the trees had to be a two-legged varmint, he told himself.

The movement came again, just a momentary shifting of shadows that could have easily gone unnoticed by anyone less observant than Longarm. His first instinct was to throw himself out of the small circle of light from the campfire so that he wouldn't be as good as a target. But the skulker might not mean any harm, and if Longarm reacted like that, it could just spook the watcher and make him run off. Longarm was more interested in finding out why somebody was trying to sneak up on him.

He forced himself to sit calmly and hoped that nobody was drawing a bead on him at that very moment. After a few minutes, when the cheroot was smoked down to a stub, he stood up, tossed the butt into the fire, and stretched like a man tired after a day in the saddle—which he was. Then he deliberately turned his back on the trees where the watcher waited, strolled over to the bluff, and opened the buttons of his pants. There was nothing more normal than a fella taking a leak after supper, he thought, so he proceeded to relieve himself against the rocky face of the bluff. When he was done, he buttoned up his pants again.

And took a long step to the side, away from the fire, ducking down abruptly as he reached some bushes growing along the base of the bluff.

The moon hadn't come up yet, and with only the faint light from the stars that were coming out to spill over the bench, he figured the watcher wouldn't be able to see him anymore. Yet his disappearance had been smooth enough, he hoped, that the gent in the trees would be mystified and wonder where he had gone. Longarm began working his way along the bench, sticking to the brush and moving on hands and knees for the most part.

The fella had to be pretty puzzled by what was going on, and Longarm hoped that puzzlement might draw him out of hiding. If it didn't Longarm wanted to be in position to circle around behind the watcher. He wanted to put an end to this right here and now and not have to worry about somebody dogging his trail all the way to Moss City.

He reached the spot where the bench narrowed down. Moving carefully, Longarm slid across to the trees and began working his way back toward the spot where he had seen the telltale movement. The campfire was still burning over by the bluff, the empty camp acting as a lure, and Longarm would be able to see if the lurker ventured out of the trees, drawn by curiosity.

It was damned hard moving through the darkness without making any noise, but Longarm managed pretty well. He'd had plenty of practice in the past; more than once, his life had depended on his ability to slip up silently on someone. He used all of those skills now, placing his feet carefully before letting his weight come down on them and moving slowly, not giving in to the impatience he felt inside. As he neared the place where he had seen the suspicious movement, he put his right hand on the butt of the Colt in the cross-draw rig.

Sliding closer, Longarm peered intently through the darkness. There was nothing moving that he could see, except for an almost imperceptible swaying of the pine boughs in a gentle night breeze. He glanced at the campfire. Nobody over there either. Had the lurker gotten away without him noticing?

Longarm took another step, and his foot came down on something alive.

He barked a curse and jerked back as the thing squirmed under his boot. Before he could bring his gun to bear on the shape surging up from the ground, something slammed into his groin and sent pain lancing through him. Longarm roared as he doubled over and staggered back a couple of steps.

Anger—and agony—turned the night red in front of his eyes. This wasn't the first time he'd gotten kicked in the balls, but that was something a man never got used to. The skulker was on his feet by now and had turned to run. By starlight, Longarm caught a glimpse of a long coat and a floppy-brimmed hat.

Even stumbling around in such piss-poor shape, Longarm could've put a bullet or two in the back of the fleeing figure. He had never been a backshooter, though, and he didn't intend to start now no matter what the provocation. Besides, he wanted answers to some questions, not a corpse. He launched himself in a dive after the man who had attacked him.

Longarm almost missed, but just before he hit the ground his arms wrapped around the ankles of the fleeing shape. The man went sprawling, and the impact of both of them landing hard knocked Longarm's grip loose. The lurker went tumbling down the slope of the hillside toward the road.

Longarm scrambled after him, trying to ignore the pain that still throbbed in his groin. He was still holding his Colt, so he jammed the revolver back into its holster. This matter was going to be settled with fists.

Half-sliding down the slope, Longarm caught up with the rolling figure and grabbed the flapping tails of the long coat. He hauled the fellow upright and sent a hard right cross slamming into the man's jaw. The would-be watcher sagged back against the hillside, limp and stunned.

That was when the hat fell off and thick, shoulder-length hair spilled down around the face of the skulker.

"Shit!" Longarm said fervently.

He had just clouted the hell out of a woman.

Now that he was supporting the figure's weight by his grip on the coat, Longarm could tell that it was lighter than a man's would normally be, unless the gent was mighty scrawny. He lowered his stunned opponent the rest of the way to the hillside, being a little more gentle now. Still, he couldn't afford to relax entirely, he warned himself. More than one female had tried to kill him in the past, and they could be just as deadly as the male of the species when they put their minds to it. Usually more so, in fact, he thought.

Stepping back, he palmed out the Colt and said, "I don't know who in blazes you are, ma'am, but I want you to get up and march up that hill anyway."

The woman let out a low moan and moved around a little as her senses began returning to her. Longarm covered her, his own senses alert for any sound or movement around them, just in case the woman hadn't been alone. Everything seemed quiet and peaceful.

After groaning again, the woman sat up and said thickly, "You didn't have to hit me! My jaw feels like it's broken."

"Well, I hope it ain't," Longarm replied sincerely. "But when folks start sneaking around in the dark, they generally get what's coming to 'em sooner or later."

"I wasn't sneaking!"

"Looked like it to me. Now, how 'bout getting on your feet?"

The woman pushed herself upright. "First you nearly stomp my ribs in, then you throw me down a hill and hit me. You, sir, are not much of a gentleman."

Her voice was vaguely familiar to Longarm, but he couldn't place it. He was anxious to see her face in the light of the campfire, so he ignored her complaint and ordered, "Up the hill. You were so interested in my fire, we'll just go have a closer look at it."

Still muttering under her breath in a decidedly unladylike fashion, Longarm's captive trudged up the slope, through the trees, and across the bench to the little blaze, which was dying down again. Longarm kicked some of the wood he had gathered earlier into the flames, and as they flared up, the garish illumination made the woman's hair look even more red than it really was. She turned angry green eyes on him as he recognized her.

"Miz Paige, what the hell are *you* doing here?" demanded Longarm.

Maureen Paige glared at him. "I was trying to figure out who you were, if you must know. I saw the campfire, and I was curious. I had no idea it was you, Deputy Long."

Longarm frowned at her. "If you were so all-fired curious, why didn't you just call out and come on into camp, like somebody who didn't have anything to hide?"

"Really, Deputy, you should know better than that." The scorn in her voice was easy to hear. "A woman traveling alone should openly approach the camp of a strange man? Wouldn't that be dangerous?"

"Maybe back East it would be," Longarm replied curtly. "Out here a gent doesn't molest a woman, no matter what sort of mean, low-down skunk he might be the rest of the time."

"Well, you can't blame me for not knowing that," Maureen sniffed. "Most of the men I've encountered haven't been such sterling examples of chivalry."

"Then I reckon you're meeting the wrong men," Longarm said. "Sit down. I've got some Maryland rye here."

"I don't want a drink!" Maureen protested.

"You will when that knot on your jaw goes to swelling up and hurting. It ain't broken, but it's going to be a mite painful."

Her hand went to her jaw and she winced, as if reminding her of the injury had made it hurt worse. As a matter of fact, Longarm saw, a bruise was already starting to show on her skin. She sat down beside the fire and said, "I still say you didn't have to hit me."

"Figured you were some gent who didn't have anything good in mind for me," Longarm told her as he picked up the bottle of Tom Moore and offered it to her. "Sorry there's no coffee. I wasn't in the mood for it, and I didn't know I was going to be having any company."

She took the bottle, eyed it dubiously for a moment, then lifted it to her lips and swallowed a sip of the rye. Shuddering, she handed the bottle back to Longarm. "If it's all right with you, I'll stick to water from that spring."

"Fine by me. Now tell me . . . what in blazes are you doing out here in the middle of nowhere?"

"I could ask the same thing of you," she replied briskly. "I was just minding my own business."

"Skulking around like some sort of Indian's more like it."

Maureen ignored him and went on haughtily. "I was traveling to Moss City and I saw your campfire. I was curious. That's the truth, Deputy Long. That's all there is to it."

"Not quite," Longarm said. "Why are you headed for Moss City?"

"I'm going there on . . . personal business."

"Personal business related to Marshal Frank Nemo?"

Maureen looked down, her features stubborn in the firelight. "I'd rather not say."

Longarm tilted the bottle of Maryland rye to his mouth and took a healthy swig. Maureen's presence was certainly an unexpected development. He wondered what she'd been up to since their encounter in Denver, weeks earlier.

Maybe he could get some information out of her by confiding some of his own. He said, "Nemo's the reason *I'm* going to Moss City. Seems another prisoner of his got himself killed while trying to escape. Not only that, but your husband and this new fella aren't the only ones to wind up like that. Nemo was town marshal for a little while in a place called Macready—"

"I know all about Ellen Haley, Deputy Long," Maureen broke in, surprising him. "Do *you* know about Bradley Hogue and Jim Morton and Sarah Devereux and Ted McClain?"

Longarm blinked. "Who are all those folks?"

"Former prisoners of Frank Nemo. Prisoners who all died trying to escape from Nemo's custody."

Longarm let out a low whistle and said, "Son of a bitch! Pardon my French, ma'am, but it sounds like you've been doing some investigating."

Maureen nodded. "Someone had to. I could tell that the U.S. marshal's office wasn't going to take any interest in my husband's death."

"I wouldn't go so far as to say that," Longarm bristled. "It's just that there was nothing to go on except for your say-so, and that's not what you'd call proof. But when the same thing happens over and over . . ."

"Six times that I know of, seven if you count the man in Moss City. Who knows how many other people Nemo murdered before he came out west from Missouri?"

"Missouri? Is that where he's from?"

"That's what he claims," Maureen said. "Or what he claimed, I should say, when he was hired as town marshal in Hastings,

73

Kansas. That's as far back as I've been able to trace him. From there he moved on to a town called Westway, then Altamont and Benson before coming to La Junta."

Longarm nodded as he considered what she had told him. "Sounds like Nemo's working his way west, all right, and killing somebody at every stop. But why's he doing it?"

"I think he must be insane."

"Could be," Longarm agreed. "But even if he is, he's still smart. He knows he can get away with that story about having to kill a prisoner who's trying to escape, but only once. If it happened again, folks might start to talk and wonder. So he comes up with some plausible reason for moving on. A lot of star-packers don't stay in one place for very long. Nothing unusual about him drifting on to someplace else."

"Where he does the same thing all over again," Maureen concluded. "It would take someone like me, who has a reason to trace his movements backward, to stumble onto the pattern."

"Or me," said Longarm. "I was planning on covering some of the same ground you've already been over. You told me your daddy was an Assistant Attorney General. You must've learned a few lessons at the old man's knee to backtrack Nemo the way you did."

Maureen lifted her chin, the stubborn expression coming back onto her face. "I wasn't going to let him get away with murdering Jack, even if our marriage was over for all practical purposes. That's just not right."

"So you found out all this about Nemo, and now you're on your way to Moss City, right?"

"That's right," she declared. "I was told he'd taken the marshal's job there, but I didn't know he had already killed a man."

"What are you going to do when you get there?"

Longarm's question brought a sudden frown to Maureen's face. "I . . . I hadn't really figured out that part of it yet," she admitted.

"If we're right about Nemo, you could've got yourself killed by confronting him," Longarm told her. "He can't afford to let anybody start spreading rumors and suspicions about him."

"No, he can't. I can see that now. I was just so outraged by what he's been doing that I suppose I wasn't thinking too clearly."

"Well, you can head on back east now. We're on to Nemo's game, and the U.S. marshal's office'll handle him from here on out."

Without hesitation, Maureen shook her head. "I'm not going to do any such thing. I have a personal stake in this, Deputy Long. My husband was one of Nemo's victims, not to mention the weeks I've spent conducting my own investigation. It wasn't easy, you know. People don't always want to answer a woman's questions."

Longarm supposed that was true. And the information Maureen had uncovered would save him a lot of time in his own investigation. Still, he didn't want to be saddled with looking out for her while he was trying to figure out what to do about Nemo.

"All this poking around you've been doing," he said. "You did that all by yourself?"

Maureen nodded. "I've always been quite independent."

Bullheaded, that was what some folks would call it, Longarm thought. He said, "It's not that smart for a gal to be traveling around out here all by her lonesome. Nemo won't be leaving Moss City in the next few days. It'd look too suspicious if he lit out so soon after killing a prisoner. I'll take you back to Denver, and you can catch a train for Pennsylvania there."

"Absolutely not! I thought you said that a woman was always safe in the West."

"Well . . . there are some gents around who're even more depraved than your run-of-the-mill owlhoot. Just to play it safe, you'd better skedaddle back to where you came from."

75

She looked at him coldly. "I don't *skedaddle,* as you put it, Deputy Long. I intend to see this matter through to its conclusion."

Longarm sighed. There was nothing much more tiring than arguing with a woman, nor more futile. Even if a fella won the argument, he lost the war more times than not. There wasn't much he could do to stop Maureen from going to Moss City short of tying her up and throwing her over the back of her horse . . .

Which made him think of something. "Where's your horse?" he asked.

"Tied up down by the road. I can go get him if you like."

Longarm shook his head. Now that she knew he didn't want her going with him, Maureen was headstrong enough to get on that horse and gallop off in the darkness toward Moss City if he gave her half a chance. He'd fetch the horse himself.

"You stay here," he said as he stood up. "I'll be back in a minute."

"Does this mean I don't have to skedaddle?" She gave him a mocking grin, but her eyes still sparkled with anger and resentment in the firelight.

"It means we'll talk about it some more in the morning," Longarm grated. "I reckon we could both use a good night's sleep."

She nodded her agreement, and Longarm went to the edge of the bench and started down the hill. He grimaced as a fresh twinge of pain went through his groin. She had landed a damned good kick on him.

Probably a good thing, he grunted to himself. Despite her hostile attitude, Maureen Paige was a mighty good-looking woman, and normally when he was spending the night alone with a good-looking woman, lusty notions just sort of popped up by themselves in Longarm's mind. And as much trouble as he was having already with Maureen, a little romping between the blankets would just complicate things that much more.

76

Longarm groaned softly. His mama back in West-by-God-Virginia would've been proud of him. She'd always said to look for the silver lining, and it took a heap of looking to find any sort of advantage to getting kicked in the balls!

Chapter 7

The night passed quietly. There were no hostile Indians in these parts, nor any other likely sources of trouble, so Longarm didn't bother standing guard. He relied on his instincts and senses honed to a keen edge by years of surviving on the frontier to alert him if there was any danger during the night.

He slept soundly until a little while before dawn, when something suddenly roused him. His eyes snapped open, and he realized that what he had felt had been Maureen Paige sliding into his bedroll with him.

"I'm cold," she whispered when she saw that he was awake. Her tone was sharp. "That's the only reason I'm here."

The pre-dawn air was a mite chilly, Longarm had to admit. Likely there was some frost on the ground, and he could see the breath pluming from his nostrils as he slid over to make a little more room for Maureen. Even with that, the quarters were pretty cramped and the two of them were shoved together tight.

Longarm glanced up at the sky and saw the gray tinge appearing to the east. The sun would be up in another hour or so, and it seemed almost wasteful to try to go back to sleep when it would soon be time to get up. He could build the fire up and start breakfast now, and if he did, they could be on the road back to Denver at first light.

It was cold outside the blankets, though, and warm inside, and he had a mighty pretty young woman snuggled up against him. There was such a thing as being too damned ambitious, Longarm thought. Nothing wrong with lying here and enjoying the warmth and closeness for a while, even if Maureen didn't particularly like him.

Not that she seemed to be quite as impatient with him as she'd been the night before. In fact, if he didn't know better he would have said that she was pushed up against him a mite tighter than she had to be. Her head with its mane of red hair was just about pillowed on his shoulder. It smelled pretty, as if she had washed it in rose water. He shifted his position slightly, and her head snuggled against him a little more, as if it was a natural thing for her to be where she was.

Her eyes stayed closed, however, and she said, "Don't get any ideas, Deputy."

"Wouldn't think of it, ma'am," Longarm told her.

To be truthful, he was getting ideas. Even fully dressed, she was warm and soft and had a smell that was part sweetness and part musk. He felt his groin tightening, and then winced as that reaction was followed by another: a twinge of pain from the area of his anatomy that had been so rudely mistreated the night before.

Uncomfortable or not, he was still getting hard. Some things truly did have a mind of their own.

Maureen wiggled in an effort to find a more comfortable position, and the movement brought her belly in contact with the erection pressing against the front of his trousers. "Deputy Long!" she gasped, lifting her head and opening her eyes. "Really!"

"If you're expecting me to apologize, Miz Paige, I ain't in the mood," Longarm said. "Remember, you're the one who crawled in here with me. I don't recollect issuing any invitations."

"But I told you, it's cold."

"Yes, ma'am, it surely is. And you kicked me in a mighty sensitive area last night while we were scuffling around, so don't think I've forgotten that. Still and all, you can't fight human nature."

"You can control it," she said sternly. "And if I damaged your . . . your private parts last night, I'm sorry, but I didn't know who you were at the time. All I knew was that something stepped on me in the dark. For all I knew, you might have been a . . . a grizzly bear."

Longarm had to chuckle. "I wouldn't recommend trying to kick a grizzly bear in the balls, ma'am, no matter whether he steps on you or not."

"You're impossibly crude," she snapped back, rolling over so that her back was to him.

That just pushed her rump up against his shaft, which was fully erect by now. Once again her breath caught in her throat as she felt it prodding her soft flesh. But although Longarm expected her to struggle out of the blankets, jump up, and flounce off, she stayed where she was, cuddled against him spoon fashion.

She released the pent-up breath in a sound that was half-sigh and half-moan. "Damn you," she whispered. "Do you know how long it's been since I felt anything like that?"

Longarm thought about Harriet Dunston. She had gone eight years without the touch of a man, and it sure as hell hadn't been that long since Maureen had known some loving. But he kept that comment to himself, knowing that she wouldn't appreciate being compared to another woman. He just said softly, "Too long, I reckon."

"I don't think I've ever . . . Jack was the first man I ever . . . the only man . . . I ought to be ashamed."

"Nothing to be ashamed about," Longarm told her. "It's

cold, and you're looking for a little warmth."

"Yes," she said breathlessly, twisting around in the blankets to face him again. "That's exactly what I'm looking for."

Then her mouth came hungrily against his, searching, wanting, finding. Her lips parted and Longarm's tongue slid between them to explore the warm, wet cavern of her mouth and duel sensuously with her tongue. Her arms went around his neck and her fingers explored the dark brown hair on the back of his head.

She raised a leg and hooked it over his thigh, and he slid his hand up the taut fabric of her pants to her hips, where he paused to knead and caress the firm flesh of her buttock. Then he moved his fingers up higher, under the tail of the shirt that had pulled out of her pants. He touched the warm skin on the small of her back and began to massage it with his fingertips, his strong fingers sending waves of pleasure through her. He could tell by the way her soft belly surged against his throbbing erection.

She reached down with one hand and closed her fingers over the shaft through his trousers, moaning deep in her throat as she did so. Longarm felt like doing a little moaning himself, especially when she let go of him long enough to unfasten the buttons on his pants and slip her hand inside. Her fingers encircled his erection, exploring the length and thickness of it.

As her hand teased him, she took her lips away from his and breathed, "I never would have believed this if I hadn't felt it for myself."

Her touch was tormenting him, but it was sweet torture. His balls still hurt some—of course they were sore after what had happened to them—but he didn't care. A man could put up with a little pain and discomfort to get what he wanted.

And Longarm wanted Maureen Paige.

His hand delved underneath her pants, tracing the cleft between her buttocks and making a shudder go through her as his fingers trailed along the sensitive flesh. Then they found the hot wetness at the juncture of her thighs and slipped into her. She welcomed him eagerly, her inner muscles clenching on the two fingers he had inside her. He left his thumb lying between her buttocks and rotated it while he reached as far inside her with his fingers as he could. The combined caresses made her gasp and bump her hips against him. Her breath rasped in her throat and came faster and faster as he continued to manipulate her. The thrusting of her hips grew frantic, uncontrollable. She clutched his erection with both hands and hung on like it was a saddlehorn and she was trying to ride a wild bronc.

Longarm waited until a series of deep shudders were spasming inside her, and then he abruptly shoved her pants down, gasped her hips, and lifted her above him. Maureen cried, "What are you—oh, my God!"

Longarm thrust up, sheathing himself inside her. She was still shaking in a powerful climax, but the strength and suddenness with which he filled her pushed her over the edge into a crazed explosion of passion the likes of which she had probably never felt before. Longarm hoped so anyway. He held on to her hips and drove himself as far as he could go, not moving much, just letting her ride him and set the pace.

Maureen was too far gone to bounce on him for more than a few seconds, though, and then she collapsed atop him, gasping for breath. Longarm stroked her flanks as a last series of tiny quivers ran through her. Despite the cold air outside the blankets, she was sweating, and a drop of perspiration beaded on the tip of her nose and fell off to splash on his cheek. Or maybe it was a tear . . .

"I never dreamed, never in my life, that it could . . . that I could . . . oh, dear Lord!" She rested her head on his broad chest while they lay still entwined below the waist. Longarm could feel the heavy beating of her heart as she lay against him. Finally, after long moments of recovery, Maureen suddenly lifted her head sharply. She realized what she was feeling and exclaimed, "You're still . . . you didn't . . ."

"Nope," Longarm said. "Not yet." He throbbed inside her to punctuate his reply.

"I'm not sure I can stand any more," Maureen protested, but he could tell she wasn't really arguing. She proved it by kissing him again urgently.

"Let's get some of these clothes out of the way," Longarm suggested.

Maureen complied eagerly. It was sort of tricky, getting their clothes off while staying inside the blankets and keeping his erection socketed firmly inside her, but they managed. When they were both mostly naked, Longarm said, "You just take it as slow and easy as you want, darlin', and I'll be ready when you are."

"All right," Maureen said as her hips began moving again, this time more languidly. For long, slow minutes she rode him, pushing her upper body up with her arms so that he could reach between them and caress the firm globes of her breasts. The sky was lightening even more with the approach of sunrise, and he could tell now that the light dusting of freckles on her face extended to her body as well. He could see them on her breasts as he cupped and squeezed them and then raised his head so that he could take each pink nipple in turn into his mouth.

The pace of Maureen's movements began to increase, and Longarm felt a growing urgency gripping him as his shaft slid in and out of her. He hoped she was getting ready for the closing gallop again, because despite what he had said, he wasn't sure he could hold back much longer.

Maureen was ready, all right. She began to cry out throatily, and Longarm felt those familiar spasms rippling through her. He abandoned any attempt at control and let his instincts take over, his hands moving from the softness of her breasts to clamp down on her thighs and hold her tightly against him as he drove into her. Any vestiges of pain were washed away in the flood of passion that swept over him, and he did some flooding of his own as his climax poured out of him and filled Maureen. When he finally relaxed, she slumped down on top of him again, sated and exhausted.

When she could talk without gasping, she said, "I ought to hate you, taking advantage of me like that."

"But?" Longarm prodded.

"But I don't. You were right, I came into your bedroll. I knew what I was letting myself in for. But it had been so long . . ."

Again he was reminded of Harriet Dunston. It seemed this was his season for making love to widow women, but Longarm wasn't complaining, not when those women were as passionate as Harriet and Maureen.

"Nothing wrong with two folks taking a little comfort from each other," Longarm said.

"No," agreed Maureen, "nothing wrong at all. But we're still faced with a problem."

"What's that?"

"You want me to go back to Denver, and I don't want to go."

That reminder of their disagreement the night before, as well as the situation with Frank Nemo, brought Longarm back to earth in a hurry. He slipped out of Maureen, bringing a brief, involuntary sound of disappointment from her, then sat up and reached for the clothing they had so hastily discarded a few minutes earlier.

The chilly early morning air made Longarm shiver as he pulled his clothes on. Maureen got dressed too, looking vaguely embarrassed. Longarm hunkered by the fire and poked the embers into life again, adding kindling until he had a small blaze going. He dug out his coffeepot and the bag of Arbuckle's and started the coffee brewing. They would breakfast on jerky and some of the biscuits he had left over from the day before.

"What is this stuff?" Maureen asked as she tried to bite off a piece of the jerky he gave her.

"Here." Longarm took the dried beef back, cut off a short strip with his pocketknife, and handed that to her. "Put the whole thing in your mouth and chew slow and determined-like. It'll soften up sooner or later. It's called jerky, by the way. Reckon they don't have it back in Pennsylvania."

"I'm sure the people there would feel deprived if they knew what they were missing," Maureen said, the words thick and a little garbled as she chewed. The sarcasm came through loud and clear, though. She seemed to be over whatever tender feelings she might have had a few minutes earlier.

The subject of which way Maureen was going didn't come up again until after they had eaten breakfast. Then she swallowed the last of her coffee and said, "You've got to make up your mind, Deputy Long. Either you can be reasonable and let me ride on to Moss City with you, or you can be an utter jackass and force me to go back to Denver."

"Considering what we did a little while ago, you ought to quit calling me Deputy Long. My friends call me Longarm."

Maureen's fair skin flushed deeply. "I'd rather you didn't remind me of that. I had a moment of weakness, that's all."

"*Several* moments, if I recollect right," Longarm said with a grin.

She ignored the jibe and said, "I suppose that given the circumstances, however, I can call you Longarm. And you can call me Maureen."

"Thanks," Longarm said dryly. "So tell me, Maureen, if I do take you back to Denver, are you going to be a good girl and stay there?"

Her chin lifted defiantly. "I will not. I'm going to confront this Marshal Nemo eventually, whether you want me to or not."

"Well, I guess there's no point in me being stubborn, is there?"

She gave him a surprised glance. "You mean you're going to let me come along?"

"I reckon so."

"Well . . ." His decision obviously left her nonplussed. "Well, thank you," she finally managed.

"You're going to have to let me call the turns when we get to Moss City, though. After all, this is the business of the U.S. marshal's office. If Nemo's been up to the sort of hijinks you told me about last night, something's got to be done about him."

"What?"

Longarm wished she hadn't asked that question, because he didn't have an answer.

He had a reason for letting her come along with him. Until he found out the truth about Nemo and decided what to do about it, he wanted to keep the itinerant lawman off balance, and the presence of Maureen—the widow of one of the prisoners Nemo had possibly murdered—could help accomplish that.

The sun was warming up now as it rose higher in the sky, and the light frost that had been on the grass was melting. Longarm stood up and said, "We'd better get riding. We ought to make Moss City by midday."

If Maureen was upset because he hadn't answered her question, she didn't say anything about it, and Longarm was grateful for that much at least.

They cleaned up after their meal, and Longarm got the horses ready to go. Maureen's mount was a chestnut mare, and Longarm had tied it not far from his own claybank after fetching it the night before. Maureen was using a regular stockman's saddle, no doubt rented from the same stable where she had rented the mare. She didn't seem to mind wearing pants and riding astraddle, so as they mounted up and started down the slope from the bench where they had camped, Longarm commented, "You must've done some riding back east."

"There were riding academies in Washington when I was growing up there, and I continued to ride after my family moved back to Philadelphia."

"Surprised that a proper young lady knows how to ride any way but sidesaddle."

She surprised him with a grin. "Who said I was a proper young lady? I'm afraid that I proved something of an embarrassment to my father on more than one occasion. A politician doesn't need a daughter who's a tomboy. He loved me anyway, and always forgave me for my . . . excesses."

Longarm chuckled. Maureen was acting friendlier since he had decided to let her come along with him, and he was glad. She was a stubborn, sharp-tongued woman when she didn't get her way, but when she relaxed he found himself liking her quite a bit.

They rode on through the morning, following the trail that wound through the foothills beside a small creek. Longarm guessed it was around ten o'clock when they rounded a bend and saw a small valley opening up in front of them. There was thick grass on the bottomlands, even this late in the year, and maybe half a hundred head of cattle milled around in a pole corral on the near side of the valley. Several riders were pushing more cattle toward the corral.

Longarm reined in and motioned for Maureen to do the same as one of the horsebackers peeled off from the others and rode toward them at a good clip. There was something familiar about the man, and as he drew nearer, Longarm recognized the stocky build and the tall white hat. He lifted a hand in greeting and called out, "Howdy, Coffee. Remember me?"

The cowhand brought his horse to a stop and grinned. "Long, ain't it? We ran into you over closer to the Kansas line."

"That's right." Longarm looked at the other riders and recognized some of them as the men who had been with Tom Coffee at that branding camp in eastern Colorado, although he couldn't recall their names. Coffee was distinctive enough so that Longarm had remembered him right away. The big deputy went on. "What're you boys doing way over here?"

"Got tired of riding for that spread over east and decided a change of scenery might be nice. You know how that is."

Longarm did indeed. During his own cowpunching days, he had quickly realized the monotony of the job. That was one of the things that had led him to go into the law-and-order business. But he knew it wasn't unusual for some cowboys, even top hands like Coffee, to drift from ranch to ranch, always looking for something they were usually destined not to find.

"Looks like you managed to keep your crew together," Longarm commented, nodding toward the other riders. "I see you've got the same boys riding with you."

"No point in breaking up a good team," Coffee said, his grin widening. He glanced curiously at Maureen, who hadn't bothered tucking her red hair underneath her hat today since she was riding with Longarm. Coffee must've wondered why Longarm was traveling with a beautiful young woman, but he was too much the gentleman to ask in her presence. Instead he said, "It'll be a while 'fore we stop for beans and coffee, but if you folks want to wait, you're welcome to share our grub with us."

Longarm shook his head. "No, thanks. We've got to be moving on. You know how far it is on to Moss City?"

"Another seven or eight miles, I'd make it. I'm not real sure because we haven't been to town much since we got to this part of the country. Been too busy out here."

"Moving the stock down from the mountains before the weather gets too bad, eh?" Longarm grunted. His eyes swept over the camp and the remains of the large fire near the corral.

"That's right. The weather's nice enough now, but it won't hold."

Longarm nodded in agreement. "Well, we'll be moving on.

Maybe we'll run into each other again if we're in these parts for very long."

"Hope so," Coffee said.

A thought occurred to Longarm. "By the way, do you remember some other gents coming along the same trail I was using, back there when we met before?" It hadn't been long after his encounter with Coffee that the would-be bushwhackers had stumbled on him beside the creek.

The cowhand frowned in thought for a moment and then shook his head. "I don't rightly recall anybody like that, but I'm not sure, Long. There some reason I ought to remember these gents you're talking about?"

"Nope, not really. I just thought you might."

Longarm didn't offer any explanation for the question, and Coffee didn't press for one. The puncher tugged the brim of his hat and nodded to Maureen, then wheeled his horse and trotted back to join his companions, who had driven the cattle into the corral along with the other stock by now.

"A friend of yours?" Maureen asked as she and Longarm nudged their horses into motion again.

"Just an acquaintance, I reckon you'd say," Longarm replied. "I was hoping maybe he could help me clear up something that happened a while back, right after my visit to Nemo in La Junta, in fact."

Longarm's brow furrowed as his words triggered a chain of thought in his brain. The attempt on his life had come suspiciously soon after his departure from La Junta, now that he came to think about it. If Nemo had some partners, or at least somebody he could get to do some dirty work for him, and if the drifting badge had decided to rid the world of a potential threat in the person of the deputy U.S. marshal who had just been told about the death of Jack Paige, then . . .

No, that was reaching too far, Longarm decided. After all, he and Nemo had faced down those bank robbers together, and afterwards, when Nemo had told him about Paige's death,

Longarm had seen no reason to doubt the local lawman's word. He had left La Junta perfectly satisfied with Nemo's explanation. That had been long before Longarm had known what a cold-blooded killer Nemo evidently was.

But if Nemo really *was* crazy, he might be so suspicious of everybody that he would think it easier to dispose of Longarm rather than risk him going back to Denver with the story of Paige's death. None of the other prisoners he'd killed in the past had been wanted on federal warrants, or at least Longarm had inferred that from what Maureen had told him.

He would have to check on that if he got the chance. Could be that Nemo's first encounter with a federal lawman had spooked him to the point of panicking and sending those gunmen after Longarm, even though murdering one of Uncle Sam's marshals was the fastest way to bring even more trouble down on a gent's head.

Well, Longarm decided, he could argue this back and forth with himself from hell to breakfast and not be any closer to an answer. But Frank Nemo knew the answers, and Nemo was up ahead in Moss City, drawing closer by the minute. Each step of the horses brought Longarm and Maureen nearer to the truth.

One thing was certain, Longarm thought—whether Nemo had sent the bushwhackers after him or not, the man was going to be damned surprised to see him again.

Chapter 8

Moss City was a good-sized town nestled in a valley at the base of Prophet Peak. Longarm saw plenty of evidence of working mines in the foothills above the settlement—smoke from the smelters, the gaping mouths of the shafts dug into the sides of the hills, and ugly mounds of tailings. To the east and south the hills were a bit more gentle and rolling, and cattle spreads such as the one for which Tom Coffee and his friends worked were located there. Miners and cowboys would mix in roughly equal numbers in the town, which could sometimes make for a volatile situation that called for a strong hand from the local law.

Longarm wondered how Frank Nemo was handling that part of his job.

There were quite a few brick buildings in Moss City, including a bank, a land development company, a surveyor's office, and a lawyer's office. Among the other businesses were a general mercantile emporium that filled an entire block, several smaller stores, a druggist, a milliner, a blacksmith shop, and two livery stables. Down at the far end of the main street were the whitewashed frame structures of the local church and school, looking not like twins but at least close relatives. And there were the saloons clustered at the near end of the street—

the Cat's Eye, the Agate, the Gem, the Lucky Seven, the Alamo, the Cougar's Den, and several smaller establishments. None of them were doing a booming business at this time of day, but conversely, none of them were empty either.

After a couple of days of eating on the trail, Longarm was more interested in finding a good restaurant or cafe, and a place called Frederickson's seemed promising. Longarm swung his horse toward it.

Maureen followed his lead, and they tied their mounts at the hitch rack in front of the cafe. As he stepped up onto the boardwalk, Longarm's eyes surveyed the street and finally found the other thing he was looking for—a sturdy frame building with a sign out front proclaiming it to be the town marshal's office. That was likely where they would find Nemo.

At the moment, though, he was ready to corral a nice thick steak, so he ushered Maureen into Frederickson's place. It was lunchtime, and the cafe was busy but not full.

They were greeted by a stout, blond, apple-cheeked woman who introduced herself as Mama Frederickson and led them to a round table covered with a checkered cloth. "You two fine young people sit down here, yah," Mama commanded. "Papa, he is out in the kitchen, and he will fix you whatever you want."

"How about a couple of steaks with all the trimmings?" Longarm asked.

Mama shook her head. "No steaks."

"Some stew?" suggested Maureen.

Again the shake of the blond head. "No stew today."

"Well," said Longarm, "what do you have?"

"Sausage," Mama declared proudly. "Good German sausage."

"Reckon that's what we'll have then," Longarm said.

Mama smiled and her head bobbed up and down. "Sausage, sauerkraut, and fried potatoes. Yah, and beer." She went off toward the kitchen, shouting, "Papa! More sausage!"

Longarm and Maureen exchanged grins. "Reckon that must be the specialty of the house," Longarm said dryly. "Hope that's all right with you, Maureen."

"It's fine," she assured him. "I had German food sometimes back in Philadelphia."

Mama Frederickson returned a few minutes later, her beefy arms loaded down with platters of food. Longarm had to admit it was good. The sausage was sizzling hot and just spicy enough, the fried potatoes were savory, and even the sauerkraut wasn't too bad, especially with the hard black bread. Longarm and Maureen washed everything down with bottles of strong, bitter German beer, which somehow tasted better than normal with this meal.

Maybe this was a mistake, Longarm thought as he polished off a second helping of sausage. Now he had to confront a potentially crazy killer hiding behind a lawman's badge, and all he really wanted to do at the moment was to loosen his pants, sprawl out in an easy chair somewhere, and take a short snooze.

Justice didn't wait for a full stomach to ease, though, so with a sigh, Longarm stood up, dropped money on the table to cover the cost of the meal, and took Maureen's arm. They waved to Mama and to a walrus-mustached, red-faced man who peered out through the kitchen door. They took him to be Papa Frederickson.

As they stepped out on the boardwalk again, Longarm nodded toward the marshal's office down the street. "That's the first place we'll look for Nemo," he said.

Maureen nodded in agreement. "And when we find him?" she asked.

"Just follow my lead," Longarm told her.

This time she didn't nod, and Longarm frowned a little as he walked down the street beside her. She had agreed to let him call the shots in their confrontation with Nemo, but he remembered how headstrong she was. She might decide to go off on some tangent of her own, and there wouldn't be much he could do to stop her. He wanted Nemo off balance but not totally spooked, not yet.

Longarm was aware of some curious glances from the townspeople they passed, but he chalked them up to the fact that he and Maureen were strangers in town and that she wasn't dressed like most of the women in Moss City. The denim pants, man's shirt, long duster, and floppy-brimmed hat might not be normal female apparel, but it was more comfortable for riding the trails, and evidently Maureen had been doing a lot of that these past weeks.

They reached the marshal's office without encountering Frank Nemo. Longarm paused in front of the door, took a deep breath, and grasped the knob. He swung the door open and stepped inside.

No one was in the office.

Longarm stood there looking around, seeing a room much like the ones Nemo had occupied in La Junta and Macready. It was a typical small-town marshal's office, with a door at the back of the room leading into the cell block.

"He's not here," Maureen said, stating the obvious.

Longarm walked over to the open cell block door and peered through it. There were four cells back there, two on each side of a short hallway. All four were empty, their barred doors standing open.

"Has he left town already?" Maureen asked, sounding rather anxious.

Longarm shook his head. "There are still papers on the desk, and I smell coffee in that pot on the stove. The place was swept out recent too, probably this morning. No, Nemo hasn't given us the slip. He's just out and about somewhere, probably tending to business."

As if to confirm Longarm's guess, the front door of the marshal's office burst open at that instant, and a man stumbled wildly into the room. It had been the man's shoulder slamming into the door that had knocked it open, Longarm realized. The stranger tried to catch his balance, but before he could do so, another figure came quickly through the door behind him and lifted a booted foot to kick him solidly in the rump. The kick sent the first man crashing into the desk and then slumping to the floor.

Longarm and Maureen stepped back hurriedly to get out of the way, and the second man stopped short at the sight of them. Longarm recognized him immediately, and evidently it was mutual, because the man exclaimed, "Longarm!"

"Howdy, Marshal Nemo," Longarm said coolly.

The man on the floor let out a groan.

Nemo glanced down at the man, who didn't seem to be in any hurry to get up, then turned his attention back to Longarm. "What brings you here?" he asked.

"Business," Longarm said, but that was all he got out before the man on the floor abruptly pushed himself to his hands and knees.

"Hold on a minute," Nemo said to Longarm. Then he palmed out his six-gun as he bent over the man he had kicked into the office. Nemo grabbed the man's arm with his free hand and hauled the prisoner to his feet. "Come on, mister," the local lawman grunted. "You got a date with a jail cell."

As Nemo shoved the man across the room toward the cell block door, Longarm asked, "Got you a troublemaker there, Marshal?"

"Just a cowboy who got a little too likkered up and started a fight in the Cougar's Den," Nemo said. "Get in there, you—"

Suddenly, the prisoner twisted out of Nemo's grasp and whirled around to plunge toward the front door. Instinctively, Longarm reached for the butt of his Colt in the cross-draw rig. He couldn't have said if he intended to halt the prisoner's flight or stop Nemo from killing the man.

Nemo used the gun in his hand before Longarm could even draw his own weapon, but instead of firing the pistol, Nemo lashed out with the long barrel, slamming it against the side of the cowboy's head before the man had taken more than one long step. The prisoner crumpled, pitching forward into a loose, unconscious ball on the plank floor. Longarm relaxed slightly as he saw Nemo holster his gun.

"Damn fool," the town marshal muttered as he reached down to grasp the cowboy under the arms. "Now he'll wake up in that cell with an even bigger headache."

"Let me give you a hand," Longarm offered as Nemo began dragging the unconscious prisoner toward the cell block. The rangy federal deputy took the man's feet, and together he and Nemo got the prisoner behind bars in a matter of moments. Nemo clanged the cell door shut and twisted a key in it.

"That'll hold him until he sobers up," Nemo declared.

Actually, the troublemaking cowboy had looked fairly sober to Longarm when Nemo booted him into the office. Sober—and scared.

As if maybe he was afraid for his life while he was in the marshal's custody?

Nemo tossed the ring of keys onto the desk and placed his hat beside them. He said to Longarm, "You were about to tell me what brings you here to Moss City." His curious gaze flickered over to Maureen. "And who this young lady is, I hope."

Before Longarm could even open his mouth, Maureen snapped, "I'm Jack Paige's widow. You remember Jack Paige, don't you, Marshal Nemo? He's the man you murdered over in La Junta!"

Damn it, there went any hope of playing this subtle-like, Longarm thought in exasperation. Still, he had halfway expected such bluntness from Maureen, and he had a glimmering of a plan to deal with it.

Nemo blinked and frowned at the accusation, and he said in what sounded like genuine bafflement, "What's that, young lady? I never murdered anybody in my life. I'm a lawman."

"Hold on, Frank," Longarm said, making his tone deliberately conciliatory. "And you, too, Miz Paige. There's no need for anybody to get all het up about this." He cast a warning glance at Maureen, then stepped over to Nemo and took the man's arm. "You see, Frank," he began, sounding almost conspiratorial now, "the young lady here is all upset about her husband getting killed when he tried to escape from your custody back there in La Junta. That's natural enough, I reckon. But when she came to the marshal's office in Denver with a story about how you were murdering prisoners, we just had to check it out, so's we could prove she's wrong. You understand that, don't you?" Longarm stopped just short of letting one eye close in a wink which would have said plainly that here was one lawman protecting another lawman.

Nemo considered what he had heard, then nodded slowly. "I see," he said. "You did the right thing, Longarm. An accusation that serious has got to be looked into." He turned his attention back to Maureen. "But I assure you, Mrs. Paige, I had no choice but to kill your husband. He was about to shoot me."

"Oh?" Maureen said icily. "What about Ellen Haley?"

Nemo lifted his left arm. "I still carry the scar where she cut me. She'd have slit my throat if she'd had the chance."

"Can you say the same thing about Sarah Devereux and Jim Morton? What about Ted McClain and Bradley Hogue?"

Longarm didn't interrupt the angry questioning, wanting instead to see how Nemo reacted to the names Maureen was throwing at him. Recognition flashed in Nemo's eyes, and Longarm knew he remembered the names.

But the Moss City marshal said stolidly, "I don't know what you're talking about, ma'am."

"Those were all prisoners you murdered while they were in your jails." Maureen's voice trembled with anger, as did her hands.

Longarm saw something he didn't like in Nemo's gaze, and he stepped forward quickly to put his hands on Maureen's shoulders. "Here now," he said sharply as he pulled her away and put himself between her and Nemo. "You can't just go slinging accusations like that around with no proof, Miz Paige. I told you I'd ride over here with you so that we could maybe put your mind at ease, but I'm not going to stand by while you tear into Marshal Nemo like that. It ain't right."

He sounded convincing enough that Maureen gave him a furious glare. Then he saw realization dawn on her face. Thankfully, she was quick enough to conceal that realization, and except for an instant, her facade of rage never slipped.

"I should have known you wouldn't really get to the bottom of this," she said. "All you lawmen are interested in is sticking together and protecting each other."

"Now there's no call for you to talk like that," Longarm began.

"Leave me alone!" cried Maureen. She jerked out of his grasp, spun around, and stomped out of the room in a perfect imitation of a woman having a hissy-fit of frustration.

Longarm was proud of her.

But instead of showing that, he sighed heavily and turned back to Nemo. "Sorry about that, Frank," he said. "Never should've brought her over here from Denver, I guess, but she made such a goddamned pest of herself, always hanging around the office and making accusations and threats." He shrugged. "I reckon I should've known she wouldn't listen to reason."

"Some folks just won't," Nemo said. "You believe me, though, don't you, Longarm? I realize some might think it looks sort of bad, the way I've been forced to kill a few prisoners when they tried to escape . . ."

Longarm waved off Nemo's explanation. "Hell, you don't have to explain things to me," he said heartily. "I know how them civilians just never really understand what it's like to tote a badge." He rubbed his jaw. "Got to admit I was a mite surprised when I heard that you'd moved up here."

"Guess I'm just too fiddle-footed for my own good," Nemo said with a sheepish grin. "I like Moss City. I've been thinking about settling down here permanently."

"Sounds like a good idea." Longarm headed for the door of the office. "Well, sorry to've bothered you, Frank."

"No bother, no bother at all."

"Reckon me and Miz Paige'll spend the night here, then start back to Denver in the morning. And when we get there, I'm going to personally put her on a train headed back East so that we can have some peace and quiet and get on about our real business."

Nemo chuckled. "You do that. In the meantime, how about having supper with me tonight? There's a Dutchy down the street who cooks up a damn fine plate of sausage."

Longarm rubbed his belly and laughed again. "I found that out already. Thanks for the offer, Frank, but I reckon I'd better keep my eye on Miz Paige instead. No telling what sort of trouble an ornery female with a head full of crazy notions might stir up without somebody to watch her."

"I suppose you're right. You be careful she don't spit blood in your eye, Longarm."

With a wry chuckle, Longarm nodded and left the office. He spotted Maureen standing on the boardwalk several blocks down the street, still holding herself stiffly as if she was angry. She was good at that pose, damned good.

But she wasn't the actor that Frank Nemo was. Nemo was one of the best Longarm had ever seen. On the surface, he was still the friendly, efficient badge-toter he had been the two times before.

But Longarm was more convinced than ever that he was also a cold-blooded killer.

Maureen didn't have much to say to him as he secured two rooms for them at the Moss City Inn, which was a substantial two-story building on the other side of the street from Nemo's office and Frederickson's cafe. The rooms were adjoining but not connecting. He put the horses in the stable out back and brought their saddles and gear up to the rooms, and when he took Maureen's things to her, she was still rather curt to him.

Longarm heeled the door of the room shut behind him and said, "For pity's sake, gal, don't tell me you were taken in by that load of bullshit I was spreading too!"

"What are you talking about?" There she went, with that defiant tilt to her chin again.

"I'm talking about the way I stuck up for Nemo," Longarm told her. "You didn't believe it, did you?"

"That's about what I've come to expect—"

"Hell's bells, you didn't give me a chance to do anything else, the way you jumped in feet first with all those accusations. I had to try to make him think I wasn't very bright, that I was just going through the motions by coming here to Moss City. Otherwise he would've closed up tighter'n a bear trap."

"Oh? And what exactly *have* we accomplished?" Maureen wanted to know.

Longarm wished she hadn't asked that, because they really weren't any closer to finding any proof of Nemo's guilt than when they had entered Moss City. Anyway, Longarm kept coming back to the fact that regardless of what proof they might find, most judges and juries weren't going to be too concerned about what Nemo had been doing. As long as the man confined his killing to known criminals, it would be difficult to do anything about him.

Maybe he ought to just gun the son of a bitch, Longarm thought disgustedly. That would take care of the situation.

But it would also make him almost as bad as Frank Nemo. Longarm knew he couldn't live with that on his conscience.

Doing things right and proper was a damned nuisance sometimes.

"Nemo knows we're here," Longarm said to Maureen. "He knows that you've dug up some of the things he's done in the past. Let's give that a chance to eat on him for a while and see what happens."

"All right," she said grudgingly. "I suppose that's all we can do right now."

Longarm stepped closer to her with a grin. "Not quite all," he said, sliding his arms around her waist.

For a few seconds, Maureen stiffened. Then she relaxed and returned his smile. "I suppose you're right," she said. "We might as well pass the time enjoyably, no matter how frustrated we are about Nemo."

"Frustration's a terrible thing," Longarm said in mock solemnity, and then his mouth came down on hers. Her arms encircled his neck and tightened. Somehow they found themselves on the bed, and then the clothes started falling away and warm flesh met warm flesh.

The rest of the afternoon passed all too quickly.

Longarm decided that two meals of the heavy German food in one day would be too much, so he and Maureen ate supper in the dining room of the Moss City Inn. Despite the passionate lovemaking which had occupied them earlier, they were barely civil toward each other in public, keeping up the masquerade that had started with their visit to Marshal Nemo's office. If Nemo happened to see them, he would think they were still feuding over Maureen's accusations.

After they had eaten, Longarm took Maureen back up to her room and said quietly to her, "I'm going to poke around town a little, have a drink in a few of the saloons."

"Why? If you have to have a reason beyond the obvious ones, that is."

"I've got a reason, all right," he said. "I want to find out how the town feels about Nemo, and the best place to overhear what I need to know is in the saloons."

She slipped her fingers under the lapel of his coat and ran them up and down for a moment. "I was hoping we could, well . . ."

"I'll be back later," Longarm assured her. "You can count on that."

"I'll come over to your room when I hear you come in."

He shook his head quickly. "No, you stay put until I come over here. You never can tell when somebody else might take an interest in me enough to do some nosing around in my room, and you don't want to stumble into something like that."

"You're talking about Nemo?"

"I'm just talking about being careful," Longarm said. "Stay in here, and don't open your door unless you know it's me standing outside. Understand?"

Maureen nodded. "All right. I'll do like you say."

"Thanks. I'll be back directly."

He left her there and strolled out of the hotel onto the main street. There were plenty of saloons to choose from, so he settled on the closest one, which happened to be the Alamo.

They didn't have any Tom Moore in the place, but the back bar was stocked with an inferior brand of Maryland rye. Better that than nothing, Longarm thought, and he nursed along a couple of shots for half an hour while he chatted with the bartender and listened to the talk in the saloon. He was able to draw out the bartender only slightly, and the man had nothing but good to say about Frank Nemo. "There's not nearly as many fights around here since Marshal Nemo took the job," the drink juggler testified.

Indeed, the Alamo was pretty peaceful for a saloon, and if what Longarm and Maureen had witnessed in Nemo's office that afternoon was any indication, Longarm could see why nobody would want to risk Nemo's wrath by starting a ruckus.

That scene and the conversation were repeated almost exactly in the Agate, the Gem, the Lucky Seven, and most of the

102

other saloons in town as Longarm made his rounds over the next couple of hours. Longarm didn't hear any real affection for Frank Nemo in the words of the townspeople, but he heard plenty of respect and even fear. Nemo was tough, no doubt about it, but a lawman had to be tough to handle a town like Moss City.

Longarm's head was buzzing a little when he called it quits for the night. He'd had quite a few drinks. He had a large capacity for liquor, but it wasn't unlimited, and he was going to be glad to get back to the Moss City Inn . . . and Maureen. He wondered what she would be wearing when he tapped on her door.

That thought, and the whiskey he'd put away during the evening, had him so distracted that he almost didn't hear the warning scrape of a foot in time.

But he did hear it, and his head snapped toward the mouth of the alley he was passing. Longarm saw a faint blur of motion, a shifting of shadows within shadows, and he heeded the alarm bells that suddenly racketed within his brain. He threw himself forward as flame geysered from the barrel of a gun, throwing an instant of hellish light over the alley.

Longarm's Colt was in his hand as he landed in the dirt of the gap between two sections of boardwalk where the alley emerged. His ears rang from the noise of the shot. More fire lanced from the depths of the alley, and the slug threw grit into Longarm's eyes as it thudded into the ground beside his head. He triggered the .44 twice, firing almost blindly, then twisted and rolled out into the street, trying to use the corner of the raised boardwalk for cover. Another slug from the alley chewed splinters from the walk.

Pawing the dirt out of his eyes with his free hand, Longarm came up on his knees and squeezed off another shot. By this time, shouts were sounding up and down the street, and a few hardy souls were running toward him to see what was happening. Longarm saw the patch of deeper darkness in the alley move and he fired again. This time he was rewarded with a grunt of pain.

He knew better than to go charging into the alley just because he'd scored a hit, though. Instead he scrambled onto the boardwalk and flattened himself against the wall of a building, waving back the townspeople who were hurrying toward him. A second later he heard the clatter of hoofbeats coming from the rear of the buildings and bit back a curse. The bushwhacker might've been wounded, but it sounded like he was still getting away.

"I'm a U.S. marshal," Longarm called. "Somebody fetch a lantern."

He wondered where Nemo was. Considering how many shots had been fired, the local law should've been rushing up by now to see what was going in.

Maybe Nemo had been here but was gone now, Longarm thought grimly. Maybe it had been Nemo lurking in that alley, waiting to kill him.

One of the townies came up holding a lit bull's-eye lantern. Longarm took it from him and ventured into the alley, holding his Colt, now fully reloaded, ready for instant use. There was nobody left to shoot at, though. The alley was empty except for a stove-in water barrel and a couple of old crates.

And a splash of blood in the dirt that showed dark in the light from the bull's-eye lantern.

"What the hell's all this?" a loud voice demanded angrily from behind Longarm as the big deputy was studying the bloodstain on the ground. Longarm turned to see the crowd at the mouth of the alley parting hurriedly for Frank Nemo.

Longarm's eyes quickly surveyed Nemo from head to foot. There was no blood visible on the marshal's clothes. Of course, he could have changed his clothes during the few minutes since the bushwhack attempt, but he didn't move like a man who'd just been ventilated by a bullet. Even a minor wound from a .44 slug was enough to shake a man up. Nemo just looked impatient to find out what had happened.

"Nice friendly town you've got here, Frank," Longarm said. "Somebody just tried to give a lead welcome."

Nemo's frown deepened. "Somebody ambushed you?"

"They did their damnedest." Longarm holstered his gun and gestured at the blood the bushwhacker had left behind. "They're the ones who wound up getting howdied, though."

Nemo shook his head. "I'm sorry, Longarm. I'll try to find out who did this." The local lawman rubbed his jaw in thought. "Could be some old enemy of yours spotted you and decided to get some revenge, sort of like back in La Junta when that bank robber recognized you."

"Could be," Longarm said.

Or it could be that Nemo had sent somebody to kill him, he thought. This could be a repeat of the attempt on his life near the Ogallala Trail.

Nemo turned to the crowd. "Break it up now, folks," he told them firmly. "Nothing to see around here, so go on about your business." He turned back to Longarm. "I'll walk with you to your hotel, just to make sure nobody else takes any potshots at you."

"All right, Frank," Longarm said mildly, keeping a tight rein on his emotions. It wouldn't do to smash that look of phony concern off Nemo's face.

At least not yet.

Chapter 9

"Somebody tried to *kill* you?"

Maureen sounded incredulous as she stared at Longarm a little later in her hotel room. He had just told her about the attempt on his life by the bushwhacker in the alley, and she jumped to the same conclusion he had as she went on. "Nemo must have something to do with this. Are you sure it wasn't him?"

"The fella I winged lost enough blood to let me know it was a fairly serious wound," Longarm said as he took off his gun rig and hung it on a bedpost. "Nemo wasn't hurt. I watched him close enough to be sure of that."

"But that doesn't mean he didn't have anything to do with it."

Longarm nodded. "The same thought occurred to me. Remember how I asked that cowboy named Tom Coffee about anybody he might've seen following me over this side of La Junta? I've been wondering if the hombres who jumped me over there were working for Nemo too."

Maureen frowned in thought. "But why would any— owlhoots, I suppose you'd call them—be willing to do Nemo's dirty work like that?"

"Been pondering on that too, but I don't have an answer yet. There's got to be more going on here than we know about."

"I just assumed Nemo was insane."

"He may be," Longarm said, "but he's smart too. I think we'd better get out of Moss City."

Maureen's eyebrows lifted in surprise. "We can't do that. We have to stay here and find out the truth."

Longarm came over to her and rested his hands on her shoulders, which were clad in a blue robe that clung to the lines of her body. He said, "We've got him spooked now, and he knows that the U.S. marshal's office is at least a mite curious about him. If he was behind that ambush tonight, he obviously doesn't want me getting back to Denver. So he's liable to send somebody else after us, or come himself if he has to."

"So we'll be acting as bait on the trail back to Denver, is that it?"

Longarm nodded grimly. "This is how come I didn't want you riding with me. I figured that sooner or later I'd have to draw Nemo out, and I didn't want you in the line of fire. Taking chances like that ain't your job."

Maureen took a deep breath and let it out in a sigh. "I admit I don't much like the idea of being a target, but if it'll stop Nemo . . ."

"There's no guarantee of that," Longarm warned her. "He might just wind up adding our names to his list of victims."

A faint smile curved her lips. "I have faith in you, Longarm."

"Well, I appreciate that," he said with a dry chuckle. "And if Nemo does send another bushwhacker after us, and if we can get our hands on the hombre and make him talk, that'll be what we need to put Nemo where he belongs."

"In jail, you mean."

"Or in the ground, if that's the way he wants to play the hand."

For a moment, Maureen looked into his eyes. Then she said,

"I'm glad I'm not a criminal, Longarm. I wouldn't want to have you after me."

"Oh, I'm after you, all right," Longarm said. "I just don't figure to arrest you." His hands moved down from her shoulders, the thumbs hooking inside her robe and spreading it apart as they descended. He bared her breasts and lowered his mouth to the insistent little nipples, sucking each of the hard nuggets of flesh in turn. Maureen closed her eyes and made a soft sound of satisfaction in her throat.

Longarm untied the belt around her waist, and she shrugged off the robe, letting it fall around her feet. He kissed the hollow between her breasts, then let his lips trail down her stomach and abdomen to the triangle of red hair at the top of her thighs. He slipped a hand between her knees and brought it up, her legs opening to his touch. She was wet and ready, he found as he nuzzled through the fine-spun red hairs. A shiver ran through her.

Longarm wasn't in the mood to wait any longer. He straightened, one arm going around her to cup her buttocks, the other pressed to her back. He lifted her, and her legs came apart and reached around him. Her hands found the buttons of his trousers and deftly unfastened them. She pushed his pants down and freed his erection from the long underwear. It was a little awkward, standing up like this, but together they managed to get everything lined up, and Maureen's breath hissed between her teeth as Longarm lowered her onto his shaft. Her ankles locked together behind his back, and the joining was complete. Neither of them could move much without putting them in danger of toppling over, but Longarm was so deep inside her that it didn't really matter. A shuddering climax began to rock Maureen almost immediately.

Holding her tightly and kissing her, Longarm tried to postpone his own climax, but her inner spasms were too much for him to withstand. He began to spurt in her, jets of wet heat that brought soft cries of delight from her each time he throbbed.

Shaken by the intensity of it, Longarm stumbled a little but stayed on his feet.

Maybe it had been over more quickly than either of them had really wanted, he thought.

But hell, getting shot at had sobered him up completely, and the night was young yet. For now, one thing they had was time . . .

Longarm slept a little later than he had intended to the next morning. He'd slipped down the hall to his own room far into the night, after Maureen had dozed off while snuggled against him in her bed and then fallen into a deep sleep. Longarm figured to catch a few winks himself, so that he wouldn't be too worn out on the trail. After all, he was counting on Nemo to either come after them himself or send somebody else to ambush them before they got back to Denver, and Longarm knew he had to be alert.

But it seemed he had barely closed his eyes when a soft rapping on his door woke him. He rolled over, grumbled a little, and looked through bleary eyes at the sunlight slanting in through gaps in the curtains over the room's single window. The sun was up and had been for an hour or two, he realized. It was later than he'd thought.

He swung his legs out of bed and reached for his pants. When he'd pulled them on, he plucked the Colt from its holster and padded quietly toward the door. Before he could say anything, a guttural voice called, "Marshal Long? You are in there, yah?"

Longarm frowned. He'd never heard the voice before, but the accent was familiar. Deciding to take a chance, he grasped the knob and pulled the door open.

The walrus-mustached cook from the cafe stood there, along with several other men. *What the hell?* Longarm thought. Looked like a whole delegation from the town had come calling this morning.

"I'm Long," he said. "What do you gents want?"

"I am Dietrich Frederickson, and these are some of my friends and fellow businessmen. We wish to lodge a complaint mit you, Marshal Long."

"A complaint about who?"

"Frank Nemo," Frederickson answered bluntly.

One of the other men said anxiously, "Keep it down, Papa. We agreed that we didn't want this getting back to him."

Longarm looked at the men and saw that they all had worried expressions on their faces. He stepped back and said, "Come on in, so that you can talk freely. I can't help you if I don't know what this is about."

"It is about Marshal Nemo," Frederickson said as he led the delegation into the room. There was no place for half-a-dozen men to sit down, so they all remained standing.

Longarm slipped his revolver back into its holster and reached for his shirt. "Tell me what's on your mind," he said.

The man who had warned Papa Frederickson to keep his voice down said, "I'm Ben Sampson, owner of the hardware store down the street. These other gents are Fred Malloy, Jimmy Riggs, Ed Larkin, Gerald Culberson—"

"No need for everybody's name," Longarm said as Sampson was getting wound up. "I likely wouldn't remember all of 'em anyway. I reckon from the looks of you that you're all businessmen here in Moss City."

"Yah," said Frederickson. "We all own businesses, and Ben, he is the mayor."

"And the rest of these boys are members of the town council," the balding Sampson added. "We're the ones who hired Frank Nemo."

"And now you're starting to wish you hadn't," Longarm guessed.

Sampson nodded grimly. "That's right. We wanted somebody tough, tough enough to keep the miners and the cowboys in line when they came into town. It used to be that not a week went by without a killing or two. That was keeping Moss City from growing the way it should, despite the fact that it's in such a prime location."

One of the other members of the delegation put in, "When there got to be enough respectable citizens in town, we decided we had to do something about the situation."

Longarm frowned. "Nemo's been here less than a month, the way I understand it. Moss City didn't grow to be such a respectable place from a helltown in that short a time."

Frederickson shook his head and said, "No, no, we had another marshal before Nemo, a good man named Will Carrington. He brought peace to our streets over the last year. But two months ago, a horse kicked Marshal Carrington in the head and killed him."

"We saw that the town was going to slip back to the way it used to be if we didn't replace Carrington with an equally tough man in a hurry," Sampson said. "It was like Providence guided Nemo here, because he showed up less than two weeks later looking for a job."

Another man said, "We hired him on the spot."

As Longarm's frown deepened, Sampson said hurriedly, "I know we should have checked him out more thoroughly, but that's not as easy as it sounds. Nemo gave us a list of the towns where he'd worked as a lawman, and his credentials were certainly impressive, even though we noticed then that he didn't seem to stay in one place for very long. When someone mentioned that, he just said that he had a wandering nature. He promised to stay in Moss City for however long it took to do the job, though."

"And he's done the job, hasn't he?" Longarm mused. "I checked out your saloons last night. Mighty peaceful. Saw an example yesterday afternoon of how Nemo deals with troublemakers too."

"Then you know why people are afraid to start trouble now,"

111

Sampson said. "Anyone who steps out of line the least bit is thrown into jail, and Nemo isn't gentle about it. Admittedly, a lot of the cowboys and miners need a little rough handling to be dealt with effectively, but there have been several instances of beatings and pistol-whippings—"

"And one prisoner killed while trying to escape."

Sampson nodded. "Yes, but that man was a newcomer to Moss City, and Nemo claimed he shot the man in self-defense during, as you said, an escape attempt. We don't hold that against him as much as we do some of the other things he's done."

Longarm debated with himself whether to tell these visitors the truth about Nemo's background and all the prisoners the renegade lawman had killed in the so-called line of duty. But he still had no real proof of his speculations, and spilling the story to Moss City's business leaders wouldn't further his own investigation, so he decided to keep the knowledge to himself for the time being. Instead he said, "You're worried that one of these days Nemo's going to get carried away and kill somebody who's important around here."

"Everyone is important," Frederickson said. "But yah, we are worried about the marshal, about whether he is, how do you say, right in the head."

Longarm figured he could've answered that too, but he didn't.

Sampson said, "When word got around town that a federal lawman was here, we knew we had to come see you. Isn't there something you can do about Nemo, Marshal Long?"

"I don't know. Looks to me like what you got here is a local matter. I'm not sure I'd have any jurisdiction over what a town marshal does." *Unless he murders some prisoners being held on federal warrants,* Longarm added to himself. But again he kept silent about that angle of the case.

"We really need help," Sampson pleaded. "We're afraid that Nemo's going to completely lose control one of these days.

Then there's no telling what he might do."

Longarm hesitated a moment, then said, "I'll take it under advisement, gents. I'm afraid that's all I can promise right now. I've got to get the lady who came into town with me back to Denver."

"And then maybe you come back, yah?" asked Frederickson.

"Maybe," Longarm replied noncommittally.

He wished he could do more for these worried townsfolk, wished he could tell them that he was even more worried about Nemo than they were. But he didn't want to take a chance that Nemo might learn just how strong his suspicions were, even accidentally. The last thing he wanted was to get Nemo so spooked that the man bolted. That would mean starting all over.

Before his visitors could protest his decision, Longarm said, "Now if you fellas will excuse me, I reckon I'll finish getting dressed and rustle up some breakfast. Mrs. Paige and I will be heading back to Denver as soon as we can."

He didn't mind Nemo knowing that. It was unlikely, Longarm thought, that the local lawman would try to set up another ambush in broad daylight as long as Longarm and Maureen were here in town. Nemo would want to wait until they were out on the trail somewhere to dispose of them. Longarm intended to make sure they were plenty conspicuous as they left town.

The delegation of businessmen didn't look pleased with his decision, but his stern demeanor as he ushered them out didn't leave them much room for argument. When they were gone, Longarm put on his boots, buttoned his collar, knotted the string tie around his neck, and shrugged into his vest and coat. He made sure the gold chain between the Ingersoll watch and the .44 derringer was looped properly between the pockets of his vest, then settled the snuff-brown Stetson on his head as he left the room and went down the hall to Maureen's room.

She was already dressed, as he had expected, but she had traded in the pants and man's shirt for a cream-colored blouse and a dark brown split riding skirt. She put on a jacket that matched the skirt and went down to the dining room with him.

"You look mighty nice this morning," Longarm told her. "Fresh as a daisy."

"You'd never know I got only a few hours of sleep, would you?" she asked with a quick, roguish smile. "Somehow I found what we were doing just as invigorating as a good night's sleep."

"Glad to hear it," Longarm said with a chuckle. He took her arm as they went into the dining room.

Frank Nemo was sitting there at one of the tables.

Maureen might have stopped in her tracks in surprise at the sight of him, had it not been for Longarm's insistent touch on her arm. "Don't let it throw you," he murmured to her, then steered their course deliberately past Nemo's table.

"Good morning, Longarm, and to you too, Mrs. Paige," Nemo greeted them cheerfully. There was a half-empty cup of coffee in front of him, along with a plate of ham, eggs, and toast. He suggested, "Why don't the two of you join me?"

Longarm could tell that Maureen wanted to reply to him, so he kept his mouth shut and let her speak for herself. "I don't think that would be very appropriate, Marshal Nemo," she said coldly.

"Well, I reckon I understand how you feel, ma'am, although I wish you could see your way clear to understanding that I didn't have any choice where your husband was concerned."

Maureen started to say something else, but Longarm stepped in then. "Sorry, Frank," he said. "We'll just take our breakfast and then hit the trail back to Denver."

"What happens then?" Nemo asked.

Longarm shrugged. "Hard to say. I'll make my report to my boss, and then it's out of my hands."

"I'm sure Billy Vail knows I wouldn't do anything under-handed."

Maureen just glared at him skeptically.

"Come on," Longarm told her. "By the way, Frank, you didn't have any luck tracking down that bushwhacker from last night, did you?"

Nemo shook his head. "There were too many horse tracks in that back alley. No way to tell which one the fella was riding when he left in such a hurry. From the amount of blood around, though, you tagged him pretty good. Could be he rode up into the hills to die."

"We'll probably never know," Longarm said. "Be seein' you, Frank."

They left Nemo to finish his breakfast and sat down at a table of their own across the room. Maureen was still casting hostile glances at the marshal of Moss City, but Longarm was pleased with the way things were going. Nemo was off balance and worried enough to be a little desperate, and that was when folks usually started making mistakes.

"It's working, isn't it?" Maureen asked as she sat down across the table from Longarm.

"I reckon we'll find out before we get back to Denver," he told her.

Chapter 10

Frank Nemo was lounging on the boardwalk in front of his office, leaning against one of the posts supporting the awning, when Longarm and Maureen rode past on their way out of Moss City a little later. Nemo touched a finger to the brim of his hat and nodded politely to Maureen, who pointedly ignored the gesture, then grinned at Longarm and called, "We'll probably run into each other again, Longarm."

"I'd count on it, was I you, Frank," Longarm replied with a grin of his own.

For all their surface friendliness, the eyes of both men glittered with suspicion, and Longarm did nothing to indicate he felt otherwise. He *wanted* Nemo to be unsure of him and the way he really felt about this situation. He wanted Nemo to be suspicious enough to make a move that would convict him in the end.

Otherwise all this playacting would have been for nothing.

Well, not exactly nothing, Longarm amended silently. There had been the lovemaking with Maureen, and that by itself had made this visit to Moss City worthwhile.

She was quite pretty in her riding outfit, but Longarm could see the strain on her face as they left the settlement behind and started down the long trail to Denver. Knowing that they had set themselves up as targets and as much as painted bull's-eyes on their backs was taking a toll on her.

To tell the truth, Longarm didn't like it much himself. But this wasn't the first time he'd set himself up as bait for some clever criminal, and with any luck, it wouldn't be the last.

The day was overcast and cool without being cold. Every now and then, the clouds would break enough to let some sunlight slant through, but those intervals never lasted more than a few minutes.

Even though Longarm and Maureen weren't pushing the horses hard, the miles rolled past beneath the hooves of the animals. At noontime, when they stopped and ate some of the sausage and hard bread they had picked up at Mama and Papa Frederickson's before leaving town, Moss City was already far behind them.

How far would Nemo let them get before he tried for them again? Longarm wondered as he ate. The skin on the back of his neck prickled at every breeze in the trees, every cry of a bird or rustle of a small animal in the brush bordering the trail. There wasn't anything much harder than waiting for somebody to bushwhack you. Even Longarm, veteran lawman that he was, could feel his nerves growing tauter by the minute.

After they had eaten and the horses had rested and been watered, Longarm and Maureen mounted up again and rode on. "This waiting is terrible," Maureen commented after they had gone a mile or so. "How do you stand it?"

"Wish I could say that it gets easier the more you've done it," Longarm told her. "But it doesn't. You've just got to keep your eyes open and hope that things turn out right."

The trail started up a fairly steep slope with a thick stand of pine trees at the top. The hillside itself was bare of brush and dotted only with a few small clumps of rocks. Longarm glanced at the trees on the crest of the ridge and felt a tingle of alarm go through him. He looked around, saw how barren of cover the hillside was, and suddenly kicked himself for not remembering this spot from the trip going the other way. To be fair about it, though, he hadn't been looking for likely places for an ambush back then.

"Wait a second," Longarm rapped out as he drew his horse to a stop and motioned for Maureen to do likewise.

She reined in and asked tensely, "What is it?"

"I don't much like this stretch of road," Longarm began. "Maybe we ought to find some other way around this ridge—"

That was as far as he got before the clouds parted momentarily again. A shaft of sunlight lanced through the opening and bounced brightly off something in the trees at the top of the hill.

"Come on!" Longarm barked, jerking his mount around in a tight circle. "We've got to get out of here!" He spurred the horse and sent it leaping back down the hill. From the corner of his eye he saw Maureen doing the same thing.

It was too late, he realized, as the clouds closed up again. They had ridden too far into the jaws of the trap. Rifles cracked at the top of the slope, and Maureen screamed as her horse suddenly faltered and then tumbled out from under her.

Longarm heard the sinister whine of bullets near his own head, but none of them struck him or the horse he was riding. He hauled the animal to a stop anyway, twisting his head around to see Maureen rolling to a stop on the ground where her falling horse had thrown her. Longarm couldn't tell if she was hurt, but a few feet away the horse was kicking its life out as blood bubbled from a couple of wounds in its flank.

Longarm flung himself from his saddle as more slugs kicked up dirt and rock splinters around his feet. "Son of a bitch, son of a bitch!" he yelped as he ran toward Maureen. He'd gotten her into this mess, though, and damned if he was going to leave her behind and run for his own life. He couldn't do that even if he hadn't been a lawman.

As he ran, he jerked his Colt from the cross-draw rig and threw some lead toward the hilltop, not having any real expectation of hitting any of the bushwhackers with the shots. He just wanted to distract the bastards for a few seconds. It seemed to work, because not as many bullets were whipping around him as he reached Maureen's side.

He jammed the revolver back in its holster and bent to scoop her up in his arms almost without slowing down. There was a small outcropping of rocks in front of them, about twenty yards away, and Longarm raced toward it. The rocks wouldn't provide much cover, but they beat the hell out of nothing, which was what he was going to find elsewhere on this hillside.

A couple of ricocheting slugs sang off into the distance as Longarm reached the rocks and dropped behind them. He wished he could have cushioned the landing for Maureen, but there wasn't time for that. Better a few bruises than some bullet holes.

He stretched her out behind the rocks and then hunkered down beside her. The outcropping extended barely six inches over their heads, and bullets were already slamming into the scant protection as the ambushers drew new beads on them. Maureen let out a moan and started to stir around, and Longarm clamped an arm across her back to hold her down.

"Stay still," he grated. "They've got us pinned down good and proper."

Maureen moaned again, then asked thickly, "Wha' happened?"

Longarm figured she had been stunned by the fall, but as he looked her over, he didn't see any blood on her riding clothes. Maybe she had been lucky too, and all the bullets had missed her. Longarm said, "They shot your horse out from under you. I don't figure you're hurt bad. Does it feel like you broke anything?"

Maureen blinked several times, and alertness came back into her green eyes. "No, I'm all right," she said, sounding more lucid. "Where are they?"

"In the trees at the top of the hill. They were sitting pretty, just waiting for us."

"Nemo?"

Longarm shook his head. "No way of knowing. All we can be sure about is that they're some fellas who want us dead."

The gunfire had settled down to a steady drone now. Longarm figured there had to be at least three bushwhackers up there to sling that much lead at them. And it was entirely possible that Nemo had sent the gunmen. Longarm and Maureen had taken their time with lunch, and anybody who knew these hills would have had a chance to circle around in front of them and set up this trap while they were eating.

"Well, your plan seems to have worked," Maureen said. "What do we do now?"

Longarm had to admire her grit. Some women would be screaming and pitching a fit with this much lead flying around. Not Maureen, though. Her eyes were wide with fright, but she had her fear under control and her voice was cool and calm.

"You're right," Longarm told her. "I reckon we've got those ol' boys right where we want 'em."

Now all they had to do was keep from getting killed while he figured a way out of this.

While the hilltop wasn't out of range of his pistol, he would have felt better if he'd had the time to drag his Winchester out of the saddle boot. As it was, he and Maureen were outnumbered, outgunned, and damn near out of luck.

Even with three rifles, it was difficult to keep up a continuous fire. During one of the brief lulls, Longarm lifted himself enough to snap a couple of shots over the top of the outcropping. He ducked back down as soon as he fired the second shot, and the ambushers opened up again. Judging from the sound of the volley, he hadn't done any damage.

Well, this hadn't worked out like he'd hoped, not at all. He had wanted to take one of the bushwhackers alive, for questioning, but it was beginning to look like he didn't have to worry about that.

The thought of surrendering himself never occurred to Longarm. Those men up on the ridge had no interest at all in taking any prisoners. They just wanted him and Maureen dead.

"The trap backfired on us, didn't it?" Maureen asked over the continuing racket of the gunfire that pinned them down. "We're not going to get out of it."

"I've never been one to give up," Longarm replied harshly. "Damned if I intend to start now." Twisting around awkwardly to keep himself behind the cover of the rocks as much as possible, he took fresh cartridges from his pocket and began thumbing them into the cylinder of the Colt.

Suddenly the gunfire increased, but something about it sounded different to Longarm. Frowning, he snapped the cylinder of the revolver closed again and looked up. Some of the shots were coming from the south, where the ridge lifted up to an even taller hill. Someone on horseback was coming down that hill, smoke drifting from the muzzle of the rifle at his shoulder as he fired rapidly.

And those shots were directed at the bushwhackers, Longarm realized, rather than at him and Maureen.

"Who the hell . . . ?" muttered Longarm.

There was no telling who the stranger was, but he was definitely not on the side of the ambushers. As the man's horse kept coming down the hillside, half-sliding, he laid down a withering fire at the would-be killers. Longarm heard a scream of pain from the top of the slope and saw one of the bushwhackers tumble loosely out of the cover of the pines, his rifle spilling down the slope in front of him.

Since the gents on top of the ridge had something else to worry about now, Longarm decided it was time he took a hand again. He said to Maureen, "Stay here, and keep your head low!" Then he scrambled to his feet and charged up the ridge. The man on horseback had reached the southern end of the hogback by now and kept up his attack, occupying the attention of the ambushers.

Longarm spotted one of the men in the trees and paused long enough to aim a shot. The Colt bucked against his palm and the bushwhacker spun around from the impact of the slug in his side. At the same time, the horsebacker flung himself from the saddle and lit running. His rifle cracked again and Longarm heard the shot echoed by another yelp of pain.

Longarm was only a couple of bounds from the top of the ridge now. He threw himself across the few remaining feet and dropped into a crouch behind one of the thick tree trunks. Aiming around the pine, he spotted the third man, who was trying to stumble down the far side of the slope toward a trio of horses that were tied in some brush. The stranger who had come to the rescue of Longarm and Maureen was beyond the third and last bushwhacker, so they had the man in a cross fire. Longarm didn't want him dead, though.

Things didn't work out that way. The stranger suddenly stepped into the path of the fleeing bushwhacker and shouted, "Hold it right there, mister!"

The ambusher cursed and jerked up his own rifle. He was wounded and slow as well as unsteady. The stranger fired even as Longarm yelled, "Don't kill him!"

His cry was too late, Longarm saw as the slug from the stranger's rifle punched into the chest of the last bushwhacker, jolting him back in a loose-limbed sprawl. Longarm could tell that the man was dead before he hit the ground.

The barrel of the stranger's rifle tracked over toward Longarm, drawn by the shout from the rangy deputy. "Ease up on that trigger, old son!" Longarm called. "I'm the gent who was pinned down behind those rocks until you came along."

"You are, eh? Well, holster your gun and step out where I can see you, mister. You'd best move slow while you're about it too."

Longarm did as he was told, slipping the Colt back into its holster and moving from behind the tree. He kept his hands half-lifted in plain sight.

The stranger came toward him, the Winchester in his hands held ready for instant use. When the two men were about a dozen feet apart, the stranger said sharply, "That's close enough. Who are you, and what's going on here?"

Longarm studied the stranger, saw a medium-tall, broad-shouldered hombre with craggy features and curly, dark brown hair under a black Stetson pushed to the back of his head. The man wore boots that had seen better days, denim pants, and a faded blue bib-front shirt. A shell belt was strapped around his lean waist, supporting a holstered Colt. The man looked like a typical grub-line rider.

"I'm much obliged to you for helping out, mister," Longarm told him. "My name's Custis Long, and I'm a deputy U.S. marshal working out of the Denver office. My badge and the rest of my bona fides are in my coat pocket, if you don't mind me reaching for 'em."

"Just do it slow and easy," the stranger warned.

Longarm complied, and he saw the stranger relax a mite once he'd exhibited the badge. The man said, "I reckon you're who you say you are." He lowered the barrel of the rifle. "I'm Walt Hudson."

"My friends call me Longarm, and I reckon after what you did, you qualify, old son."

Hudson grunted. "Why'd those men want to kill you? They outlaws of some sort?"

"Let's take a look and see if we can find out. First, though, I want to tell the lady who was with me that she can rest easy."

Hudson's bushy eyebrows lifted, and he said, "There's a woman with you? I couldn't tell that. All I saw was some

123

folks pinned down, and I figured I'd better take a hand."

"And we're mighty glad you did," Longarm said. He went to the edge of the trees and called down the slope, "It's over, Maureen! You can come on up here."

He saw her stand up and wave to him to signify that she was all right. Feeling a surge of relief that they had both made it through the ambush relatively unharmed, Longarm turned back to Hudson. "Let's see who those boys were."

They went first to the man Hudson had just shot, since he was the closest. The dead man was lying on his back, his arms flung out to either side of him, his contorted features frozen in a grimace of pain. There were several days' worth of beard stubble on his lean face, and he was dressed in nondescript range clothes. His hat had fallen off, but it was just a brown Stetson, somewhat stained and worn. All in all, there was nothing to distinguish the bushwhacker.

And Longarm had never seen him before in his life.

At least not that he could remember, Longarm amended. It was possible he'd passed the gent on the streets of Moss City without paying any attention to him.

"Know him?" Hudson asked.

Longarm shook his head. "Nope. Wish I did. Let's check on the other two."

They were just as dead and just as much strangers to Longarm, he found a few minutes later after he and Hudson had taken a look at both of the corpses. Longarm felt anger and disgust growing in him. He wouldn't be getting any information out of the ambushers, and he had counted on that to establish a solid link with Frank Nemo. He was no closer to proving Nemo's villainy than before.

Longarm heard Maureen coming toward them, and turned away from the corpses to meet her, hoping to shield her from the worst of the blood and death. She was pale but didn't seem too shaken as he went to join her.

"Are they all dead?" she asked.

Longarm nodded. "That's the way the hand played out. Wish it hadn't, but there's not much we can do about it."

Walt Hudson strode up to them. He glanced at Maureen and asked Longarm, "Your wife?"

Before he could answer, Maureen said, "I can speak for myself, and no, I'm not Deputy Long's wife. My name is Maureen Paige. Thank you for helping us, Mister . . . ?"

"Hudson, Walt Hudson." The cowboy tugged on the brim of his hat. "You're welcome, ma'am. I'm just glad I happened along when I did."

The three of them started down the slope after untying the horses that had belonged to the dead men, leaving the bushwhackers where they had fallen. Longarm asked, "Where were you headed, Walt?"

"A place called Moss City. Ever heard of it?"

Longarm and Maureen exchanged a glance. "We just left there this morning," Longarm said. "It's a little more than half a day's ride west of here." He hesitated. "Got business there, do you?"

"You could say that," Hudson answered shortly.

"Mind if I ask what it is?" The instincts Longarm had developed over years as a lawman warned him that Hudson's answer might be important.

"Well, maybe I shouldn't admit this," Hudson said slowly, "what with you being a star-packer and all . . . but I'm going there to kill a man. A man named Frank Nemo."

Chapter 11

The flames of the campfire crackled and danced merrily in the night. Walt Hudson stared into them as he sipped his coffee and said, "Ellen Haley was my sister. She married a gent who was a banker in Independence, Missouri. Everything was going along fine for them until Ellen's husband decided to do a little speculating. Problem was, he did it with the bank's money."

"And it turned out he wasn't much of a speculator," Longarm guessed.

Hudson nodded. "That's right. I'm still not sure why I'm telling you all this, Long, but I reckon it's because Ellen's dead now and so is her husband. Can't either one of them be done any harm anymore." He sighed. "The only reason Ellen got mixed up in that phony stock certificate scheme was to try to help Charles get back the money he'd lost. But Charles got caught, and Ellen knew it was only a matter of time before the law came after her too. She ran. She came to me for help, but there was nothing I could do. I didn't have the kind of money she needed to set things right."

"So she kept running, until Nemo spotted her in Macready and arrested her," Longarm said.

"And then killed her." Hudson's voice was filled with bitterness. "Maybe if I'd been able to do something when she came to me . . . I've got a little horse ranch in Kansas, but hell, it's mortgaged to the hilt already, and I was cash poor. Still, I should've been able to do *something* . . ."

Longarm wanted to tell Hudson to quit kicking himself, but getting somebody else to give up his guilt was one of the hardest things in the world. That decision was one that had to be reached on his own or it would never do any good.

"What happened to your brother-in-law?" asked Maureen.

Hudson laughed humorlessly and shook his head. "Charles? He hung himself in his jail cell less'n a week after he was arrested. Ellen had already left Independence and I don't know if she ever found out about it. I sort of hope she didn't, because I know she would've grieved for the son of a bitch, and he wasn't worth one of her tears, not a single one."

Longarm didn't want the discussion to get too maudlin. They still had to figure out what to do about Nemo—as well as what to do about Hudson's vendetta against the renegade lawman.

To get things back on track, he said to Hudson, "So when you heard about your sister's death, you set out to track down the fella who killed her."

"It was the only thing I could still do for her," Hudson replied grimly. "I left the running of the ranch to my foreman and came out here, but by the time I got to Macready, Nemo was gone. It's taken me this long to pick up his trail again, but I heard he was in Moss City and started there right off. That's where I was headed when I ran into that bushwhack attempt on you two."

"What an incredible coincidence," Maureen murmured.

"Not really," Longarm said with a shake of his head. "Nemo's arrogant enough so that he hasn't been trying to hide his trail, and he's pulled enough of these stunts that he was bound to draw some attention sooner or later." He grinned at Hudson.

"We were mighty lucky you came along when you did, though, Walt, else we'd probably be buzzard bait right about now."

Hudson frowned. "I'm not sure I understand. What is it that ties the two of you to Nemo?"

Quickly, Longarm explained the events of the past few months, and Maureen added the facts she had uncovered about Nemo's background. Longarm concluded by saying, "I'm pretty sure Nemo's not even his real name. I think he picked it out of a book called *20,000 Leagues Under the Sea*."

Hudson shook his head and said, "I wouldn't know about that. And I don't care what the bastard's real name is, when it comes down to it. I just want him dead. I know good and well he murdered my sister. Ellen wouldn't have tried to escape."

"She ran from Independence rather than be caught there," Longarm pointed out.

"She ran, but that's all. She was sweet-natured, Long. That's what got her in trouble in the first place."

Everything that Hudson had said about his sister fit the pattern for Nemo's victims, Longarm thought as he sipped his own cup of Arbuckle's. He said, "Maybe you're right. But that doesn't leave us any closer to proving what Nemo's been up to."

"You think he sent those bushwhackers after you?" asked Hudson.

"I think it's likely," Longarm replied. "I don't know of anybody else who'd want to get rid of me right now, and Maureen's not a threat to anybody except Nemo. If those gents had killed us, they could have stolen our money and gear, and it would have looked like we were murdered by some robbers. There wouldn't be any evidence to tie the killings to Nemo. Then, after a while, he could leave Moss City and drift on, free to start the whole thing all over somewhere else."

"Where'd he get the men to come after you?"

"From the look of those corpses, they were hardcases who'd kill a man for a little *dinero* with no questions asked. It might have been enough just to promise them whatever they could find on our bodies."

Hudson nodded, his brow still creased in thought. "It all fits together, I reckon. I'm no lawman. Puzzling out these things is pretty much beyond me."

Longarm didn't tell him that there were still some unanswered questions. Something about the whole situation still didn't quite ring true to Longarm, but he couldn't put his finger on what was missing.

They had left the dead bushwhackers on the ridge. Longarm hadn't been in any mood to bury them, and neither had Hudson. It had been an impulse of the moment to join Hudson on his trek back to Moss City, but now Longarm was glad he had made that decision. A vague plan was forming in his head to replace the one that hadn't worked out earlier.

Now they were camped about ten miles from Moss City. Longarm leaned back on an elbow and said, "So you intend to go on into town tomorrow and kill Nemo, is that it?"

Hudson's face stiffened into a taut mask. "I knew I shouldn't have told you. What are you going to do, Long, arrest me? I haven't done anything yet. And when I do face Nemo, it's going to be a fair fight."

Longarm held up a hand to forestall any more angry protests from Hudson. "Wait just a minute," he said. "Let's eat this apple one bite at a time, Walt. I just want to tell you that I've seen Nemo in action. He's pretty fast on the draw. And you don't strike me as any sort of fancy shootist, old son. No offense."

"I get by," Hudson said stiffly. "I can handle a gun."

"I'm sure you can. But it won't avenge your sister's death a damn bit for you to go get yourself killed. Wouldn't it be better to bring the son of a bitch to justice?"

"How can I do that?" asked Hudson. "You know how it is, Long. He's a lawman. Folks are always going to take his word for it when he says a prisoner was trying to escape."

"Unless we can prove he's been lying by working together."

Maureen glanced sharply at him. "I thought we were going back to Denver."

"We would have . . . if we'd managed to take one of those bushwhackers alive so that my boss could question him and get to the bottom of this."

"Nemo might still send some more men after you when those three rannies don't come back to let him know the two of you are dead," Hudson pointed out.

"He might," Longarm admitted. "But I reckon there's a better way to get the goods on him."

Maureen frowned and asked, "Are we setting ourselves up as bait again?"

Longarm shook his head. "We've got some better bait now, if ol' Walt here goes along with us."

Hudson sat up straighter. "Wait just a minute. What are you talking about, Long?"

"I'm talking about giving Nemo enough rope to hang himself," Longarm said with a grin. "And he can't dance on air soon enough to suit me."

Two days later, Walt Hudson rode down the main street of Moss City. He hadn't shaved, and trail dust lay heavy on his clothes. He knew he looked rather hard-bitten, and that was exactly how he wanted to appear.

Since parting company with Longarm and Maureen, he had spent the time camped in the hills well outside of town, waiting until Longarm had had time to put the first part of the plan into motion. The whole scheme seemed pretty complicated to Hudson, but as Longarm had explained it step by step, it sounded as if it had a good chance of working.

Hudson hoped that was the case. Vengeance ought to be a simple thing, he thought. In a world that was fair, he would kill Frank Nemo, just as Nemo had killed his sister.

But the world wasn't fair, never had been. And sometimes the best way to get to where you were going lay in a round-about direction.

Hudson angled his horse toward the hitching rail in front of the Agate Saloon. It was late afternoon, and there were quite a few horses tied at the rack. Hudson added his mount to their number and then stepped up on the boardwalk. He pushed through the batwings into the shady interior of the Agate.

The long mahogany bar ran down the right-hand wall of the saloon, and the space to the left was filled with tables. A few card games were going on, and billiard balls clicked on the table at the rear of the room. There was a piano on the left-hand wall, but it was silent at the moment. The saloon had a music of its own, though, a melody comprised of talk and laughter, the whisper of cards being dealt, the clink of bottle against glass.

A horse-faced bartender came up to wait on him as Hudson leaned on the hardwood. "What'll it be, mister?" the drink juggler asked.

"Whiskey to start off," Hudson told him. "And then a bucket of beer."

"This is a high-class joint, friend," the bartender told him with a grin. "We don't serve our beer in buckets."

"I don't care what it's in, just bring it," growled Hudson, glaring across the bar at the man.

"All right, all right, no need to get angry about it," the bartender said as he poured a shot and shoved it across the bar. "I'll get your beer." He reached for a gleaming glass mug on a back-bar shelf.

Hudson lifted the whiskey to his lips, tossed it back, and then abruptly spewed out the liquor. "Goddamn!" he cried. "What kind of shit is this? I asked for whiskey, you son of a bitch, not skunk piss!"

The convivial conversation in the saloon began dying away fast at the disturbance. The bartender's long features were set angrily as he said to Hudson, "Look, friend, there's nothing wrong with that whiskey. And you'll pay for it even if you did spit it out."

"We'll see about that," Hudson grated. He reached for the mug of beer the bartender had drawn from a keg. "Let's find out if the beer in this place is as bad as the whiskey."

For a second, the bartender looked as if he wasn't going to surrender the mug, but then he pushed it over to Hudson, obviously hoping that this stranger to Moss City would be satisfied with it and stop making trouble. However, Hudson's nose wrinkled in disgust before he even tasted the beer, and when he had taken a sip of the brew, he announced loudly, "That's even worse than the whiskey!"

With a flip of his wrist, he threw the rest of the beer right in the bartender's face.

As the shocked bartender staggered back, pawing at his beer-drenched eyes, Hudson yelled, "Nobody tries to cheat Walt Hudson, you bastard!" He threw the mug across the bar, shattering the mirror over the back bar.

Several men leaped up from nearby tables and lunged toward him. Hudson whirled around to meet their charge, keeping his hand away from his gun as he did so. He didn't want this to turn into a shooting scrape. He slammed a fist into the face of the nearest man, knocking him backward. The townie stumbled into a couple of his companions, and all three of them went down in a tangle of arms and legs.

Another man managed to grab Hudson around the shoulders and drive him back against the bar. Pain jolted up Hudson's spine from the impact, but he ignored it as best he could and hooked a punch into the belly of the man who had hold of him. The man's breath gusted in Hudson's face as the blow landed. Hudson brought up his other fist and clipped his opponent on the point of the chin. The man's teeth clicked together as he fell backward.

"Get the son of a bitch!" the horse-faced bartender yelled furiously as he reached below the bar and came up with a bung-starter. With several of the citizens of Moss City crowding around the troublemaking stranger, the bartender couldn't swing the weapon.

Fists thudded against Hudson's body as the saloon patrons took their shots at him. He reached out and grasped one man's vest, yanking hard and pulling the man toward him. Hudson twisted and heaved, and the man flew past him and over the bar to go crashing to the floor behind the hardwood. That half-turn exposed the back of Hudson's head to the angry mob and a clubbed fist caught him there, setting off brilliant fireworks in his brain.

He didn't want to be knocked out. It was important for him to stay conscious. With a roar of rage, he flung his arms out, clearing a small space around him.

That move backfired, because now the bartender had room to swing the bung-starter. Hudson's instincts warned him, and he jerked his head aside just in time to avoid a blow that might have cracked his skull. Instead the bung-starter smashed against his left shoulder and made his entire left arm go numb. Gasping in pain, Hudson stumbled forward.

He used that momentum to his benefit as the men closed in around him again. He lowered his head and drove forward like an angry bull, butting one of his opponents in the stomach. The man doubled over and went backward, and Hudson ran past him.

"Stop him!" the bartender shouted. "Don't let him get away! Somebody fetch the marshal, dammit!"

There, that was what he'd wanted all along, Hudson thought. They'd been mighty slow to raise the cry for Marshal Nemo.

The lawman must have become aware of the commotion in the Agate some other way, because as Hudson forced his way through the ring of men around him and broke out into the open, he saw a man wearing a badge appear at the door of the saloon. The badge-toter slapped the batwings open and hurried in, gun in hand. For an instant, Hudson's brain, hungry for vengeance, screamed at him to grab his own gun and start blazing away at the sandy-haired lawman.

If he did that innocent people might be killed, and there was no guarantee Nemo would die. Hudson couldn't even be sure this was Nemo he was facing, because he had never seen the man before.

"Watch out, Marshal!" yelled the bartender, confirming the newcomer's identity at least. "He's crazy!"

Nemo leaped forward, the gun lifting in his hand as he prepared to bring it down on Hudson's head. Hudson grabbed Nemo's wrist before the blow could fall. He had to make this look realistic.

That wasn't a problem. With his free hand, Nemo slammed a punch into Hudson's stomach. Hudson tried to maintain his grip on Nemo's gun wrist, but the marshal was too strong. Nemo ripped his hand free and then slashed at Hudson's head with the long barrel of the gun he held. The weapon smacked against the side of Hudson's skull.

More rockets exploded behind Hudson's eyes. He groaned as he felt the muscles in his legs turn watery. He grabbed the front of Nemo's shirt in an attempt to stay upright, but the marshal struck again with the gun. This one was only a glancing blow, but a part of Hudson's brain was still working well enough to tell him that he'd better fold his hand right now unless he wanted Nemo to kill him. He let himself fall, crumpling into a heap at the feet of the local lawman. He moaned again and lay still, allowing himself to drift into a half-conscious state.

"Take him over to the jail," he heard Nemo say, although the marshal's voice sounded like it was coming from miles away. "Throw him in one of the cells. He won't be going anywhere for a while."

As strong hands grasped Hudson and hauled him to his feet, he heard Nemo ask the bartender, "What happened here, Horace?"

"I don't know, Marshal. This fella asked for whiskey and beer, and then he sort of went crazy. I never saw such a thing."

"Well, we'll see if he's got enough money in his pockets to pay for the damages. Until then, he can sleep it off behind bars . . ."

Nemo's voice faded away as Hudson was dragged out of the saloon and into the street. The tips of his boots left furrows in the dust as the townsmen who had hold of him hauled him over to the jail. He was aware of being taken inside and dumped on a hard cot in one of the cells, but after that things went black for a few minutes.

He sensed that not much time had passed when his faculties returned to him. He dragged several deep breaths into his body, wincing at the twinges of pain in muscles already sore from the beating they had taken in the fracas. The front door of the marshal's office slammed as someone came in, and Hudson lay still, his eyes closed, as footsteps came into the cell block.

"Might as well wake up, boy," Nemo said as he paused outside the cell. "I know I didn't hit you that hard."

Hudson groaned. "Hard enough, you son of a bitch," he said gutturally. "My head feels like it's stove in."

"You'll live," Nemo said. "Sit up and let's have a look at you."

Hudson managed to swing his legs over the side of the cot and pull himself upright. His head was pounding, and he lifted his hands to his temples as he glared at Nemo. He couldn't have said what he'd expected the man who killed his sister to look like. Nemo was an ordinary enough gent, except for that meanness around his eyes.

"What's your name, boy?" the lawman asked.

"I don't have to tell you that," Hudson responded.

Nemo shrugged. "Don't really matter. I know your name. You yelled it at Horace over there in the Agate. It's Walt Hudson."

"What of it?" Hudson asked in surly tones.

"Oh, nothing. It's just a name that sounds a mite familiar to me."

Hudson felt a surge of excitement. Nemo's recognition of his name meant that Longarm had carried out his part of the plan. Now all they had to do was wait and see how Nemo played things.

"Seems to me like I got a wire about a fella named Hudson," Nemo went on in a deliberately casual tone. "Actually, it was a bulletin sent out to all the local peace officers in this area from Marshal Vail in Denver, about how a shotgun guard named Walt Hudson made off with a U.S. mail pouch a week ago. That pouch happened to be full of bearer bonds. Last time he was heard of, Hudson was headed in this direction." Nemo's face hardened. "You're a damned fool, Hudson. With that much loot, you should've kept going. And if you were going to stop, you sure as hell shouldn't have picked a fight in a saloon."

"I don't know what you're talking about," Hudson said coldly. "I never heard of any of this."

"We'll just see about that," Nemo told him. "I'm going over to the telegraph office right now and wire Marshal Vail that I've got you in custody. I imagine he'll send somebody to pick you up right away. You just stew in that awhile, Hudson. You could've gotten away . . . if you weren't stupid."

Nemo stepped out of the cell block and shut the heavy wooden door that separated it from the rest of the office. Hudson heaved a sigh and leaned back against the wall behind the cot.

So far, so good.

Nemo brought Hudson some supper that night, sliding the tray through a slot in the bars, but the marshal didn't have much to say. Neither did Hudson. He maintained his surly silence when Nemo came back to get the tray.

"How's your head?" Nemo asked just before he left the cell block. "You thinking clear again?"

"Clear as ever," Hudson growled.

"Well, you better improve on that. Your time's running out, Hudson. I wired Denver, just like I told you I was going to. Marshal Vail said he'd have a man here to get you in a couple of days."

Nemo went out, and Hudson allowed himself a small grin.

By morning Hudson's headache had subsided. He hated being cooped up like this, though, even if it was part of the plan Longarm had hatched. Hudson had never been in jail in his life until now, and it wasn't an experience he wanted to repeat any time soon.

Assuming he got out of this alive, he reminded himself. Things could still go wrong, and he might wind up dead. It was a risk he was willing to take if it meant getting his revenge on the man who'd killed Ellen.

Nemo was in a cheerful mood as he came into the cell block. The marshal was whistling an off-key tune. He stopped in front of Hudson's cell and grinned at the prisoner.

"Good morning," he said. "Sleep well?"

"Why the hell do you care?"

"Oh, you'd be surprised how much I care about my prisoners, Hudson. Just because I'm a lawman doesn't mean I can't sometimes take a liking to the folks I arrest. Like you, for instance."

"Yeah, I'm sure you care a whole hell of a lot," Hudson said sarcastically.

"I do," insisted Nemo. "And I'd hate to see you have to go to prison for that robbery. I checked through all my reward dodgers, Hudson. You're not wanted for anything else, are you?"

Hudson wasn't sure where Nemo was going with this questioning, but Longarm had warned him to be on the lookout for anything unusual. Maybe this sudden solicitude on Nemo's part qualified for that description. Hudson decided to play along with him.

"That was the first job I ever pulled," he said, lowering his head and staring down at the stone floor of the cell. He let a sheepish tone creep into his voice.

Nemo chuckled. "Pretty good haul for a first-timer. Beginner's luck, I guess."

"I reckon."

"Think you might go straight if you had a second chance?"

Hudson let his head come up. "I'd sure as hell try to," he vowed, letting his instincts guide him through this maze.

"Well . . ." Nemo's voice dropped into a conspiratorial tone. "I know a way you could get that second chance, Hudson. But it'll cost you."

"Are you talking about a bribe?"

For a second, Hudson thought he had made a fatal mistake with the blunt question. Nemo's eyes narrowed, and his mouth became a tight, grim line as he stared through the bars at the prisoner. After a moment he said, "I don't like that word, mister, not one damn bit. What I'm talking about is a chance for you to go straight, but I'll be damned if I'm going to let anybody profit by their lawlessness if I can help it." Nemo hooked his thumbs in his belt. "I'll lay my cards on the table, Hudson. Your only chance of getting out of this is to turn those bonds over to me."

"And you'll let me go? I'm paying you to let me escape?" Hudson wanted to make sure everything was clear before he agreed to go ahead.

Nemo laughed harshly and shook his head. "Hell, no. You'll be paying me to kill you."

Hudson's eyes widened in surprise. He wasn't sure he had heard Nemo correctly. "Pay you to kill me?" he exclaimed. "What in blue blazes . . ."

"Take it easy," Nemo said sharply. "Just shut up and listen, Hudson. If you escape from this jail cell, you'll still be on the

138

run. That federal warrant will still be hanging over your head. The only way you can get out from under it permanently . . . is by dying."

"Seems mighty drastic to me," Hudson said.

"You wouldn't really be dead, you damned fool. Here's the way it works. You give me those bonds, and I find some drunk or drifter who fits your general description. *He's* the one who gets killed trying to escape. Walt Hudson winds up dead and buried, and you give yourself a new name and go on your way, without ever having to worry again about that old robbery charge."

Hudson's pulse pounded in his head. As he had told Longarm, he was no detective, but even he could see the pieces falling into place now. Nemo was no crazy killer but a cold, cunning criminal instead. For a fee, he provided a means of permanent escape for prisoners who had enough loot to pay him off.

But that meant his sister Ellen might still be alive somewhere, living under a new name, and the same was true of Maureen Paige's husband.

Hudson reined in his excitement, trying hard not to let it show on his face. He couldn't let Nemo tumble to the fact that his story was a phony.

He pretended to think over Nemo's offer for a moment, then nodded his head. "All right," he said. "It sounds good to me, Marshal."

"I thought you'd see the light, Hudson. Now all you have to do is tell me where you've got those bonds stashed."

Hudson shook his head. "Not so fast. If I tell you that, you could grab the bonds and still turn me over to the federal boys. I want out of here first."

"Sort of a case of you trust me and I trust you, eh?" Nemo said with a grin. "All right, I reckon we can do it that way. Besides, I'd rather conduct our business after dark. Less prying eyes that way." Nemo squared his shoulders. "Tonight, I'll let you out and you can get those bonds for me. Just don't try and pull some sort of double cross."

"Don't worry about that, Marshal. I figure it's a small price to pay for not having to look over my shoulder for the rest of my life."

"Now you're getting smart. I'll bring you some breakfast."

Hudson leaned back against the wall and sighed when Nemo had left the cell block. Longarm's plan had worked like a charm so far. Nemo's secrets were out in the open now, and all that was left was to bring him to justice.

Chapter 12

Longarm walked out of the telegraph office in Boulder and linked arms with Maureen, who had been waiting for him on one of the benches just outside the door. "Did you get in touch with Marshal Vail again?" she asked.

He nodded. "Yep. I wired Billy that everything was going according to plan, so far as I know anyway, and he sent word back that Nemo got in touch with him last night. Hudson got himself thrown in Nemo's jail, just like we planned, and Nemo recognized his name."

"I'm a little worried about Walt," Maureen said with a frown. "He seemed like a nice man, and he's taking an awful chance."

Longarm inclined his head in acknowledgment of her point. "Hudson knew it was going to be risky, and he wanted to go ahead with it anyway. Reckon he's willing to take a few chances to help us get the goods on Nemo. But I got to admit, Billy wasn't crazy about the idea of bringing in a civilian either. He'd have rather waited until we could send another deputy in instead. But I don't reckon Hudson would've waited, and he could've spoiled everything by barging into town for a showdown with Nemo. This way we've got him on our side."

"I suppose you're right. I just hope Nemo hasn't hurt him."

"Ol' Walt struck me as the sort of gent who can take care of himself. He did all right when those bushwhackers had us pinned down."

Three days earlier, Longarm, Maureen, and Hudson had ridden into Boulder, the biggest settlement between Moss City and Denver. Longarm had burned up the wires sending messages to Billy Vail, recruiting the chief marshal's assistance in putting the plan into motion. Vail had sent the wire to Nemo in Moss City, wording it so that it sounded like a message sent out to all the lawmen in the area, when in truth it had gone only to Nemo. Longarm hoped that the renegade star-packer would bite on the bait contained in the telegram and arrest Hudson, but Hudson had agreed to cause some sort of disturbance in town, just to stack the deck and make sure he drew Nemo's attention.

Then all Hudson had to do was stay alive and find out what Nemo was really up to, because Longarm was now convinced there was more to this whole matter than a lawman who had gone kill-crazy.

Yep, Longarm thought wryly, that was all Hudson had to do.

Now that things had had time to be set in motion, he would ride back up to Moss City and lie low near the town, keeping an eye on the jail as best he could. Despite what he had said about Hudson choosing to run the risk of being arrested by Nemo, Longarm was worried about the man too, just like Maureen. He wanted to be close by in case Hudson needed a hand.

"Your room at the hotel is paid up," Longarm told Maureen as they strolled down the boardwalk from the telegraph office. "You can stay here while Hudson and I wrap things up in Moss City."

"I'll do no such thing," Maureen said without hesitation. "I'm going back there with you. I'm going to be in on the end of this."

Longarm frowned. He had halfway expected this argument from Maureen, but he had hoped she would show more sense. He said bluntly, "I'm liable to have my hands full, and I can't be looking out for you."

"Nobody asked you to. I've done pretty well looking out for myself so far."

He couldn't argue that point. But he wasn't going to concede either. "Look, this is law business," he said stubbornly. "You've helped a whole heap already, Maureen. Without you, we might not've ever found out the truth about Nemo. But now it's time for you to let me and Hudson handle the rest of it."

"And if I don't?"

"Then I'll have to ask the sheriff here in Boulder to hold you on the charge of interfering with a federal officer in the course of his duties."

She stopped short on the boardwalk and stared at him. "You'd do that?" she asked. "You'd actually do that after . . . after all we've been through together?"

Longarm wasn't sure if she was talking about the time they'd been shot at or the lovemaking they'd done, and it didn't really matter either way. "I'm sorry," he told her. "But you ain't giving me a lot of choice in the matter."

She studied him for a long moment, her gaze cool but intent. "You really are the dedicated lawman, aren't you?" she murmured. "You don't let anything stand in the way of your job, not emotion, not anything."

"I try not to," Longarm said honestly.

"Have you ever given any thought to a career in politics? I think they could use a man like you back in Washington."

Longarm couldn't help but grin. "Afraid I don't lie well enough for that. I reckon I'm satisfied for now being a deputy marshal."

"Well, that's a pity." Maureen sighed. "I suppose it's pointless to argue with you, however. I'll stay here, as you asked."

"Thanks," he said, nodding. "I'll get my gear together and start back to Moss City."

She came up on tiptoes and let her lips brush his. "You be careful, Longarm. Do you hear me?"

"I'm always careful," he told her. "How do you reckon I've lived *this* long?"

After bidding farewell to Maureen, Longarm collected his horse and saddle and gear from the livery stable near the hotel and started up the road to Moss City. If he didn't run into any trouble, he would reach the vicinity of the town late that afternoon. He planned to find a spot in the hills near the settlement where he could keep an eye on the jail through the field glasses in his saddlebags. Come nightfall, he'd slip into town and see if he could talk to Hudson through the barred window of the cell. He hoped that by then Hudson would have the proof they'd need to arrest Nemo.

Longarm had spent a great deal of time pondering Nemo's activities, trying to figure out what the man's real motives were, but he wasn't any closer to an answer. For all he knew, Nemo was just a lunatic, plain and simple.

But Longarm's gut told him otherwise. The only reason Nemo would have had to send bushwhackers after him was if Nemo had something *else* besides the deaths of his prisoners to conceal . . .

Longarm was so deep in thought as he rode along the edge of the foothills that he didn't notice the hours passing or fully appreciate the beauty of the late fall day. Soon the cold and snow and ice of winter would settle down over the Rockies and the rest of Colorado, but today the sky was clear and the sunshine still held a hint of warmth in it. Folks without so much on their minds would be enjoying the good weather while they could, but Longarm had other things to think about.

Creases began to appear in his brow as he kept the horse trotting along at a good pace. Normally he was pretty thorough when it came to the cases he worked, but this one had been spread out over a couple of months and hundreds of miles. It had been interrupted too by other assignments, and he'd had to concentrate on those jobs for a while. But now he tried to shove all the distractions out of his mind as he sent his thoughts back to the first day he had met Frank Nemo, over on the Ogallala Trail in La Junta. The day that a bank robber had recognized him and thrown down on him, spooked into action even though Longarm hadn't really been paying any attention to him . . .

Longarm jerked his horse to a stop. "Well, son of a bitch!" he exclaimed aloud.

The sudden revelation that had dawned on him saved his life in the next instant, as a bullet fanned his face. The sound of the shot drifted down from his left.

Longarm didn't wait to see where the ambush was coming from this time. He snatched his hat off his head and slapped his mount's rump with it, sending the horse leaping forward into a gallop. There were more shots, but the bullets didn't come close enough for him to hear them.

Up ahead of him, the road curved to the northwest between two hills. Longarm didn't like the looks of it, but when he glanced over his shoulder, he saw that a couple of riders had appeared on the trail and were spurring after him as fast as their horses could carry them. The bushwhackers weren't going to take a chance this time. They'd lost at least three men and maybe four in their previous attempts, and their numbers might be getting thin.

Longarm leaned forward over the neck of his horse and urged the animal on to greater speed. Over the pounding hoofbeats, he heard more shots and looked back to see powder smoke drifting up from rifles in the hands of his pursuers. Well, they'd have to be damned lucky to hit him, firing from the backs of galloping horses that way, but Longarm hated to count on that, especially the way this case had been going.

At the same time, he knew he had nobody but himself to blame for some of his troubles. He had looked, but he hadn't seen. And now he was paying the price for that.

He jerked his gaze back to the trail in front of him, and slowed abruptly as he saw more riders moving into the gap between the hills. They were coming from the opposite direction, and they were led by a stocky rider in a bright-colored shirt and tall white Stetson. Even a hundred yards away, Longarm recognized him.

Tom Coffee.

Longarm jammed the heels of his boots into the flanks of his mount and drove it forward again. His surprise at seeing Coffee and the other men had lost him some valuable time, and the men chasing him had closed up the gap a little. When Longarm looked back, the slugs from their rifles were kicking up dust barely a dozen yards behind him.

He glanced ahead again and saw Tom Coffee and his men yanking Winchesters from their saddle boots. They weren't far from him now, and he could see the grim expressions on their faces as they watched him flee from the bushwhackers. Coffee held up a hand and called, "Hold on there, Custis! What the hell—"

"Tom!" whooped Longarm. "I'm damned glad to see you, old son! Those sons of bitches are chasing me—"

Longarm slowed his horse momentarily as he called out to Tom Coffee. Coffee and the other cowhands were only a few feet in front of him now, blocking the trail, but the bushwhackers were charging on anyway, even though they had stopped shooting.

Longarm saw Coffee suddenly lift his rifle. That was what Longarm had been waiting for. He jabbed his horse's flanks again and sent the horse plunging ahead. At the same time

Longarm whipped out his Colt and snapped a shot at Coffee. The cowboy ducked and grated a curse, then jerked the Winchester up and fired, but he was too late. Longarm shot another man out of the saddle and slammed through the line of riders.

He knew he had little chance of escaping, but the knowledge that Walt Hudson was sitting there in Nemo's jail, waiting for his help, made Longarm at least try to get away. A storm of lead sang around Longarm's head as Coffee and his companions opened up on the fleeing deputy.

Something slapped Longarm's left shoulder like a giant hand, and he knew one of the bullets had clipped him. He felt himself sagging in the saddle and grabbed the horn to steady himself. He twisted and threw a couple of shots behind him, not really expecting them to do any good.

They didn't. Instead, a finger of fire traced its way across his forearm, and the pistol slipped from fingers suddenly numbed by the bullet crease.

Longarm felt the horse stumble underneath him. He knew it had been hit by one of the shots, but the animal was game and kept running.

An instant later, he heard the thud of another bullet against horseflesh, and he kicked his feet out of the stirrups as the horse pitched forward. Longarm threw himself to the side, landing hard on the ground and rolling over and over. The impact knocked the breath out of him.

"Hold your fire! Stop shooting, damn it!"

The shouted orders came from Tom Coffee. Longarm had come to a stop lying face down. He gulped some air into his lungs, tasting dirt along with it. He heard the horses of the cowhands circling around him.

Circling like a bunch of damned vultures, Longarm thought bitterly.

"Don't try anything, Custis," Coffee warned. "That was a damned slick move you made. You like to ventilated me."

147

Longarm looked up and glared at the man, who was sitting with his hands crossed on his saddlehorn, wearing a smug expression. "Wish I had plugged you, you son of a bitch," Longarm spat out.

"No need to talk like that. We've shared a campfire a time or two, Custis. I was hoping we could do this friendly-like."

Longarm pushed himself into a sitting position, then hauled himself to his feet. The two bushwhackers who had chased him down the trail had joined the group surrounding him. It was obvious now they were all part of the same bunch. Longarm recognized some of the men from his previous meetings with Coffee, but most of them were strangers. Coffee had himself a good-sized crew . . . but it was smaller now than it had been before they started trying to kill Longarm.

"Those were your boys that first day, over by the Ogallalla, weren't they?" he demanded as he frowned up at Coffee. "You shared your Arbuckle's with me, then sent a couple of men after me to kill me."

Coffee shrugged. "I recognized your name. Custis Long, the U.S. marshal they call Longarm. The hombre who busted up the Laredo Loop and went into Robber's Roost and came out alive. The fella who's tangled with every sort of owlhoot from the Rio Grande to the Milk River. Hell, Longarm, like it or not, you're famous."

"So naturally, when I came up to your camp that day, you figured I was after you and your pards."

"Well, shoot, what was I supposed to think?" demanded Coffee. "Nobody has a branding fire that big in a fall roundup. I had to figure that you knew we were blotting brands."

Longarm wanted to keep Coffee talking. So far he hadn't seen any way out of this predicament, but as long as Coffee was running off at the mouth and explaining things, Longarm was still alive.

And as long as he was alive, he wasn't going to give up hope.

"When the rest of your crew came in, you sent a couple of them after me," Longarm prodded. "They caught up to me at that creek, but I managed to kill both of them."

"We found where you buried 'em later," Coffee admitted. "I thought you'd come after us again, but that was the last we saw of you for a while. I didn't know how come you'd decided to leave us alone, but we weren't just about to turn down any good luck. We moved our operation over here to the west while we had the chance." The boss rustler grinned and added, "Some of the boys wanted to hunt you down and gun you just on account of the fellas you killed at that creek, but I talked 'em out of it. Business and revenge don't always mix."

Longarm didn't bother explaining why he hadn't tried to break up Coffee's cattle-stealing ring. Truth to tell, he hadn't known anything about it. Sure, now that he thought about it, he remembered from his own cowboying days that branding was relatively rare during a fall roundup. But even if he'd thought about that during his first encounter with Coffee's bunch, it would have been one hell of a leap of logic to conclude from that evidence alone that they were wide-looping.

Coffee's guilty conscience had made that leap, though, and the resulting attempt on Longarm's life had started a long chain of events that had kept him off balance and muddied his thinking. He'd been too quick to blame everything bad that happened on Frank Nemo.

Well, he knew better now . . . not that the knowledge was going to do him a damned bit of good.

Coffee was saying, "When we didn't see hide nor hair of you for a while after coming west, we were sure we'd given you the slip, Custis. It was quite a shock when we ran into you again a few days ago."

"You figured I was still on your trail, I reckon," Longarm said. "Ever wonder why I didn't just go ahead and arrest you, if that was the case?"

"I thought you might be looking for more evidence against us. All I knew for sure was that we couldn't afford to take a chance."

"So you sent a man into Moss City to shoot me from an alley," Longarm accused.

"And you killed him instead," Coffee replied, his face growing taut with anger. "That made three of my boys you'd put under. I couldn't let you get away with that, Custis."

"So next time you sent three more, and they wound up dead too."

"Thanks to that rannie who butted in," grunted Coffee. "Who the hell was he anyway?"

"Just some grub-line rider who saw an uneven fight and pitched in," Longarm said, keeping Walt Hudson's identity to himself for the time being. He didn't want any of the rustlers to try to seek revenge on Hudson in the future.

Assuming that Hudson lived through the tricky scheme designed to ensnare Frank Nemo.

Longarm took a deep breath. He needed to get out of this mess so that he could hurry on to Moss City and protect Hudson, but if he didn't, at least Maureen and Billy Vail knew the story. If Nemo killed Hudson, Vail would act, sending in a dozen federal marshals if he had to.

Of course, that wouldn't do Hudson a hell of a lot of good . . .

"Look, Coffee," Longarm said, "I don't know if you'll believe me or not, but I ain't the least bit interested in your cattle stealing. That's a state crime, not a federal one. My only gripe with you boys is the way you keep trying to bushwhack me. Why don't you ride on while you've got the chance and not make things worse for yourselves by killing a federal officer?"

Coffee chuckled. "You must take me for a fool, Custis. Are you saying that if we let you live, you won't turn us in or come after us yourself? You don't really expect us to believe that, do you?"

"Well, I was hoping, old son," Longarm said with a sigh.

Coffee shook his head. "Sorry, Custis," he said as he lifted his pistol. "I liked you, I really did. Be a shame to kill you—but I got to do it."

Longarm tensed, ready to leap toward one of the other men and try to get his hands on a gun. But before either he or Coffee could do anything, a rifle cracked from the hill to the south.

Coffee cried out in pain as the bullet struck him in the left shoulder. Longarm was moving even as the boss rustler was falling out of his saddle. Leaping forward, Longarm reached out and closed his hand over the barrel of Coffee's gun. The other cow thieves couldn't fire without hitting their leader, and those precious few seconds of hesitation gave Longarm time to wrench the pistol out of Coffee's hand.

With his other hand, Longarm reached for the horn on the saddle of Coffee's nervously dancing horse. He swung up as he reversed the Colt and let the butt settle into his palm. The other men were opening up on him now that he was mounted and Coffee was sprawled on the ground. "Kill the son of a bitch!" Coffee screamed as he clutched his bloody shoulder.

Longarm fired as a bullet whipped past his head, and had the satisfaction of seeing one of the wide-loopers fly out of the saddle. Another one fell, and Longarm knew that his mysterious benefactor was still scoring. He had no idea who was up on the hill helping him; the last time he'd been caught in a situation similar to this, it had been Walt Hudson who pitched in. Hudson was still in jail in Moss City, though, unless something completely unforeseen had happened.

There was no time to ponder the question. Longarm whirled the horse around, snapped off two more shots, then drove his heels into the animal's flanks. It leaped forward, racing down the trail toward Moss City. The rustlers were milling around behind him, still shooting at him but not pursuing. A couple of them were trying to help the wounded Tom Coffee to his feet, Longarm saw as he threw a glance over his shoulder.

He knew it would be only a matter of moments before the gang came after him, so he made the most of his time and got all the speed he could out of the horse. It was a sturdy black stallion, and its long legs covered the ground with amazing rapidity. It made sense that Coffee, as the leader of the rustlers, would have the best horse.

Longarm was counting on that. It gave him a chance, however slim it might be, to get out of this mess.

He heard gunfire crackling behind him, but no more shots were coming from the ridge where his rescuer had opened up on the wide-loopers. The trail curved sharply, and as Longarm put the horse through the turn, he felt a surge of hope. He was out of sight of his pursuers, at least for the moment, and he recalled that the road between here and Moss City had quite a few of these curves as it followed the easiest path through the rugged foothills.

Maybe he could reach Moss City before they caught up to him, he thought. If that was the case, the members of the gang might fall back and make a run for it, rather than risk chasing him all the way into town.

Suddenly, out of the corner of his eye, he spotted movement to his left. Turning his gaze in that direction, he saw a single rider galloping toward the road at an angle, taking the sometimes steep slopes at a dangerously breakneck speed. The horsebacker's intent was clear—he intended to intercept Longarm up ahead.

For a moment, Longarm thought the rider was one of the cow thieves, but then he realized that the man was probably the one who had bailed him out of the jam he'd been in. The stranger had turned to the north and cut across some hills, intending to intersect Longarm's route. It looked like the plan was working too, because the rider was drawing inexorably closer to the road.

"Son of a bitch!" Longarm burst out when he recognized the riding outfit on the stranger, who wasn't a stranger at all.

His fat had been pulled out of the fire by Maureen Paige.

He kept the black at a hard gallop as Maureen drove her chestnut down the last slope and veered onto the trail beside him. There was no time to ask questions now, but Longarm looked over at her and nodded his thanks, seeing how pale and shaken she looked. But she kept her horse racing along beside his mount, never flinching or breaking stride. Side by side, they dashed through the twists and bends of the trail, and every few minutes the rustlers reappeared behind them, whooping and shooting until another turn in the road took their quarry out of sight.

Now it was up to the horses galloping beneath them, Longarm knew. The horses—and luck.

Chapter 13

One thing Walt Hudson had told Marshal Nemo was true—
he'd never been in jail before.

And after spending a night and a day behind bars, Hudson
was convinced he never wanted to again. There was something
about being locked up like this that made a man's skin crawl
and his nerves get itchy. Hudson wasn't sure how hombres
who had to serve long prison terms kept from going completely
mad. One thing was certain—jail must have affected his sister
Ellen for her to have agreed to a scheme like the one Nemo
had proposed.

But it would be over soon, he thought as he looked out
the small, barred window and saw the sun setting, turning
the sky orange and purple and deep blue. Soon the gray
shadows of dusk would begin to gather, and once night had
fallen, Longarm would show up.

Hudson had quite a story to tell the big deputy. With the
testimony Hudson could provide, there was more than enough
evidence to arrest Frank Nemo.

And once the renegade lawman was in custody, maybe he
could be forced to tell where the criminals he had helped to
escape by arranging their "deaths" were living now. Of course,

Nemo might not know where all of them could be located, but at least there would be a starting place.

Hudson sighed and went back to the cot, stretching out on its hard surface and putting his hands behind his head. He frowned as he thought about the implications of Nemo's pending arrest. If Nemo spilled everything he knew, it could mean that Hudson's sister Ellen would be captured and brought back to face justice for her part in the scheme her late husband had hatched, as well as for being an accessory to the murder of whoever Nemo had killed in her place. Hudson hated that part of it. But he was convinced that Nemo couldn't be allowed to continue getting away with what he had been doing. For one thing, the crooked marshal had been murdering innocent people to substitute for the prisoners he had allegedly killed. No way around it, Nemo was a cold-blooded murderer.

He was doing the right thing by helping Longarm, Hudson told himself. And speaking of Longarm, the deputy ought to be showing up soon, he thought as he sat up.

He stood and went back to the window. The sky was gray now except for a narrow band of red on the western horizon, the last lingering effects of the sunset. Where the hell was Longarm, Hudson asked himself silently. But then he told himself to relax. It was early yet. Longarm wouldn't want to make his move before it was good and dark.

Hudson just hoped Nemo felt the same way. He didn't know what he'd do if Nemo demanded to be led to the non-existent bearer bonds before Longarm arrived on the scene.

It began to look like that was going to be the case, however, because the cell block door swung open and Nemo strode in, jingling a ring of keys from his left hand. His right rested on the butt of his Colt, Hudson saw as he turned away from the window. It was growing dark in the cell block now, except for the light that spilled in from the marshal's office out front, but that was enough illumination for Hudson to see that Nemo wasn't taking any chances.

"You just stay there against the back wall of the cell, friend," Nemo said as he thrust one of the keys into the lock on the cell door. "I'd purely hate to have to shoot you before we've concluded our deal, but you know I'll do it if I have to."

"Don't worry, Nemo," Hudson assured him. "I want out of here as bad you want me out. I'll cooperate."

Nemo twisted the key and opened the door, stepping back quickly as he did so. He palmed out the Colt. "Just a precaution, you understand," he said with a faint grin. "Besides, if anybody sees us, it'd look mighty strange if I wasn't holding a gun on you. But we shouldn't be bothered. I've got your horse and mine out back. You can take me right to those bonds."

Hudson was thinking furiously, trying to decide what to do next. He didn't want to get too far from the jail, because that was where Longarm would come looking for him. As an idea occurred to him, he said, "We won't need horses. We can walk to where the bonds are hidden."

Nemo's eyebrows lifted slightly in surprise. "Is that so? Well, come on, take me to 'em." He motioned impatiently with the barrel of the gun.

Taking care to keep his hands in plain sight, Hudson stepped out of the cell. He kept some distance between himself and Nemo too, just so the marshal wouldn't get spooked. Nemo backed into the office with the gun in his hand still trained on Hudson. With his free hand, he motioned for Hudson to follow him.

"Go through that door over there," Nemo ordered, pointing to a small door at one side of the room.

Hudson opened it and found himself in a narrow corridor. He realized that the hallway ran alongside the cell block and led to the building's rear door. With Nemo behind him, he went to the back door and grasped the knob.

"That's right," Nemo said. "Out into the alley."

Hudson opened the door and stepped out into the darkness, every nerve in his body stretched taut as he did so. For an instant, he thought about making a break, but he discarded the idea quickly. Longarm had told him that Nemo was good with a gun, and the marshal had made it plain that he wouldn't hesitate to shoot down his prisoner if he had to.

Nemo followed him into the alley and shut the door, cutting off what light came down the hallway and plunging the alley into deeper shadows. Hudson could barely make out the nearby bulks in the darkness that were the saddled horses Nemo had mentioned.

"Now," the marshal said quietly, "where are those bonds, Hudson?"

"Just a minute," Hudson replied, trying not to be too obvious about the fact he was stalling for time. "I'm sort of turned around. This is the first time I've been back here. Which way's the livery stable from here?"

He wasn't sure where the question about the livery stable had come from, but it was as good as any, he supposed. Nemo grunted and said, "Livery stable, eh? It's down the street to your left."

"That's where we're going," Hudson declared, getting a firmer grasp on the story he was going to tell. "I hid the bonds in there when I stabled my horse."

"Do tell. Well, get going. We ain't got all night. You want to be well on your way before morning, don't you?"

Hudson started walking slowly down the alley with Nemo following him. "What are you going to do about, you know, getting somebody to take my place?" he asked.

"Somebody to die for you, you mean?"

Hudson felt a shiver go through him at the cold callousness of Nemo's response. He'd seen some hard times and run up against some bad men in his life, but never had he encountered a rattlesnake in human form like Frank Nemo. Longarm had said that Nemo got his name out of some book written by a

Frenchman, but as far as Hudson was concerned, Nemo was a character out of another book, the Good Book. Nemo was Satan himself.

Trying to rein in his wildly spinning thoughts, Hudson said, "It's hard to tell where I'm going. It's dark, and like I told you, I've never been back here before."

"Don't worry, we're almost there. The stable's got a back door, and I happen to know that the old man who runs it goes to sleep with the chickens. He'll be pounding his ear in the office up front, and he'll never know we're there."

"I hope not."

"You let me worry about that," Nemo snapped. His normally affable exterior was changing the closer they got to what he thought was a fortune in bonds.

Hudson walked on for a few more yards, stumbling a little in the thick darkness. Then Nemo said, "That's far enough. Here's the stable."

Looking up at the dark bulk of the building looming next to him, Hudson said, "Yep, I reckon it is."

"Do you see the door? Open it up."

Hudson fumbled along the wall until he found the door. It had a simple latch holding it closed and wasn't fastened in any other way. He lifted the latch and let the door swing out at him.

"Inside," prodded Nemo.

Hudson gritted his teeth and walked into the stable, which was dimly lit by a lantern with its wick trimmed low that hung on a post extending from the front wall of the barn. What was he going to do now, he wondered. He had to come up with something to keep Nemo occupied . . .

"The bonds are up in the hayloft," he said, pitching his voice in a whisper so as not to disturb the sleeping liveryman. "I stashed them up there earlier."

"Well, go up and get 'em," Nemo said impatiently. "Once you've turned them over to me, you can go back down the alley, get on your horse, and ride out of here. I'll take care of everything else."

Hudson nodded, feeling a touch of eagerness for the first time tonight. It had just occurred to him that he might find a pitchfork up in the hayloft. That would make a dandy weapon, and maybe he could throw it down and catch Nemo peering up the ladder. He stepped over to the ladder that led up to the hayloft and grasped one of the rungs.

Hudson had pulled himself up only a couple of steps when Nemo said abruptly, "That's far enough."

Holding himself stock still on the ladder, Hudson swallowed. He had heard the deadly menace in Nemo's voice. He said, "What's the matter, Marshal? I thought you wanted me to get those bonds."

"They're not up there, and you know it, Hudson. You tried to get tricky and outsmarted yourself, and I've been playing along just to see how far you'd go with this." Nemo's voice grew even colder. "I brought your horse down here myself after I'd locked you up. You never even set foot in this stable until now, and we both know it."

There was a ball of fear and sickness in Hudson's stomach, but he tried to ignore it. He forced himself to say, "Well, hell, Marshal, you don't expect me to just turn over all that loot, do you? After all the chances I took to get it?"

"So you *were* planning to double-cross me!" Nemo's voice lashed at Hudson, whose grip tightened on the ladder.

"Look," Hudson said, "the bonds are buried in an oilcloth pouch outside of town. I can take you right to the spot, especially if you're willing to wait until daylight, so that I can see where I'm going. No tricks, Marshal. You've got my word on it."

"No, I don't think I can trust you anymore, Hudson." Something new had crept into Nemo's voice, a tone of outraged betrayal. A shiver went through Hudson at the sound of it. Nemo went on. "You're just like any other goddamned owlhoot, always ready to bribe a lawman or lie to him or anything else you have to do to escape from justice. You're not the first one who's done something like this, you know."

"I . . . I'm not?" Hudson forced the words out of his mouth, sensing that he had to keep Nemo talking if he wanted to live.

"There were others who took me up on the offer. Each of them turned their dirty money over to me, even knowing that I was going to kill somebody else to take their place. Hell, they never even hesitated! They were perfectly willing for somebody else to die just so they'd be safe. And you're just like 'em, Hudson, just like 'em."

"No, I'm not!" Hudson said desperately. He wasn't a cowardly man, but something about Nemo made his flesh crawl. "I just wanted a second chance. You don't have to make it look like I was killed. Nobody has to die! You can still have the bonds if you just let me escape. I'll take my chances after that."

Slowly, deliberately, Nemo said, "No, I can't do that. I'm not sure there *are* any bonds. Anyway, I don't care anymore. I've got plenty of money. The others paid me well . . . before I killed them."

Hudson tried to lick his lips, which had gone completely dry, but his tongue was too thick and awkward. He managed to say, "But they didn't really die. You just made it look like they were dead."

Nemo laughed, and it was an ugly sound. "That's what they all *thought* was going to happen. They thought their money could buy them anything. They died looking shocked as all get out, when I took their money and then killed them anyway."

Hudson felt like someone had just punched him in the stomach. It was obvious now that his sister Ellen was dead after all. Nemo had killed her, just like Hudson had thought all along . . . until this morning. Then he had grasped the slim hope that Ellen was still alive.

160

But she was dead, dead at the hands of this madman. Like all the others, she had fallen victim to the crooked marshal. Nemo had come up with a cunning plan to make money, all right, but when you got right down to it, he was still as crazy as a bedbug.

And one hell of a lot more dangerous.

"It's a shame you managed to break out of jail and ran up here to try to steal a horse for your getaway," Nemo continued. "But luckily, I caught up to you in time. I found you and warned you to stop, but you wouldn't. So I had to shoot you. That's the story I'll tell."

Hudson heard the unmistakable sound of Nemo easing back the hammer of the pistol, and knew that in the next moment a slug would crash into his back as he clung to the ladder. He would fall to the floor and die there, and Nemo would have one more helpless victim to chalk up to his account.

The hell with that.

Hudson turned his head and asked bluntly, "You don't think Longarm will fall for that story, do you?"

"Longarm!"

The mention of the federal deputy shocked Nemo enough to make his finger ease off the trigger for a second, just as Hudson had hoped it would. Hudson flung himself sideways off the ladder, diving toward one of the stalls. Nemo's gun thundered, the bullet knocking splinters from the ladder as it struck where Hudson had been only an instant earlier. Hudson landed on the floor at the head of the empty stall, sliding on the mixture of straw and horse piss and shit that coated the planks. Nemo fired again, but Hudson had already scrambled to his feet and darted into the shadows of the big barn.

"Come back here, you son of a bitch!" Nemo yelled furiously.

Hudson skidded to a stop in a patch of thick darkness, hoping that any sounds he had made were obscured by the stamping and blowing of the horses stabled here. The animals were spooked by the deafeningly loud gunfire. Hudson tried to catch his breath. The shots would rouse the old man who ran the livery, as well as some of the other townspeople. If some of Moss City's citizens showed up, Hudson could give himself up. If he was surrendering in front of witnesses, Nemo couldn't gun him down in cold blood—although the marshal was crazy enough that it was hard to predict exactly what he *would* do. Hudson knew he had to survive the next few minutes and hope that Longarm showed up soon.

Nemo would know, however, that he couldn't afford to let Hudson live. Hudson's reference to Longarm had been a double-edged sword. It had bought Hudson the second he needed to leap out of the line of fire, but at the same time he had revealed that he knew too much already about Nemo's activities. Hudson swallowed the despairing curse that sprang to his lips. The hand was too far along now. It had to be played out.

A thin, querulous voice called from the front of the livery, "What in blazes is goin' on back there?"

Nemo answered, "It's me, Josh, Marshal Nemo! I'm after an escaped prisoner. Run get me some help, damn it!"

"Lordy, Lordy! I'm goin', Marshal!"

Hudson winced as he listened to the exchange. A moment later, he heard the slam of the office door as the old liveryman hurried out into the night, yelling at the top of his lungs about an escaped prisoner. That was a smart move on Nemo's part, Hudson knew. Knowing there was a deadly fugitive in the barn and that a gunfight was going on, most of the town's citizens would stay back. They wouldn't force their way in to see what was going on. For a few minutes, anyway, Nemo would have a free hand to hunt him down in this cavernous structure.

And once Hudson was dead, nobody in Moss City would challenge Nemo's story, at least not seriously.

Hudson felt around in the straw, searching for something—anything—he could use as a weapon. There was nothing, not even an empty bucket. Maybe he could slip over to the back door again, he thought. If he could get into the alley, he could run down it to those saddled horses and leap on one of them to gallop away. But first he had to reach the alley.

There was a sudden clatter of breaking glass, and a red glow sprung up. "Son of a bitch!" Nemo yelled, loudly enough for anyone outside the barn to hear. "The bastard's set fire to the livery!"

Hudson bit back a groan. Nemo was going to drive him out with flames and blame the destruction on him. A dead man couldn't deny the accusation, and Nemo intended for Hudson to be dead very shortly.

Hudson broke and ran toward the back door as the blaze Nemo had started by breaking the lantern raced through the straw-filled stalls. Horses shrieked and whinnied in pain and terror as they smelled the smoke and felt the heat from the flames. The interior of the barn was rapidly filling with smoke, and Hudson hoped the chaos would help conceal his flight.

Nemo was waiting for him, though. Hudson saw the marshal from the corner of his eye, looming up on his left. The gun in Nemo's hand boomed, and Hudson felt the bullet smash into his side. The impact spun him around. He fell heavily, tried to get up, and slipped. Weakness spread through him like the fire was spreading through the stable.

"It's all over, Hudson," Nemo said as he strode toward the wounded man. Hudson saw him coming but couldn't do anything about it. His muscles no longer responded to the commands of his brain, and his whole left side was wet with blood. He looked up as Nemo loomed above him, lit from behind by the flickering flames.

"A funeral pyre like this is more than you deserve," Nemo grated as he cocked his pistol for the finishing shot. The light from the fire cast a hellish red glow over his features.

Satan himself, Walt Hudson thought.

Then a gunshot boomed, and another and another, and that was all Hudson knew as darkness claimed him.

163

Chapter 14

Somehow, Longarm and Maureen Paige had managed to stay ahead of their pursuers during the long run to Moss City, but Longarm could feel Tom Coffee's black stallion beginning to falter beneath him. If such a fine horse was wearing down, then Maureen's mount had to be on its last legs. The animal was game, though, just as game as its rider, and Maureen kept up with Longarm for the most part.

Night had fallen as they galloped along, and now as they swept around a curve and saw the road falling away down a slope, the lights of the settlement appeared in the little valley in front of them. "Come on!" Longarm called to Maureen, his spirits buoyed by the sight. "We're almost there!"

He still expected Coffee and the others to fall back when it became obvious that they weren't going to catch up to their quarry in time. But he and Maureen weren't out of the woods yet, Longarm realized as he sent the black horse pounding down the long slope toward the town. This stretch of the trail was a straightaway, and the gang of rustlers would have their best chance yet to either close the gap or bring them down with rifle fire. As Winchesters began to spang and crack behind them, Longarm leaned forward over the neck of his horse to make himself a smaller target, and motioned for Maureen to do the same.

A glance over his shoulder showed him that the pursuers had come closer than at any time since this desperate race had begun. There was enough light from the rising moon for him to make out the dark forms behind them, and he also saw the orange flashes from the muzzles of their rifles.

Nemo was going to be damned surprised to see him again, Longarm thought with a grim smile. Especially if Coffee and his companions *didn't* turn back as Longarm expected.

The hillside down which the trail descended was becoming more gentle now, and the outskirts of Moss City were only about half a mile away. Longarm checked on the pursuit again. It was going to be close, too damned close.

But he was convinced they would have made it if Maureen's horse hadn't stumbled.

She let out a frightened cry as the horse's gait faltered. For a second its hooves pawed frantically at the ground as it tried to regain its balance. Longarm jerked his head around and saw the situation. He yelled, "Kick your feet loose from the stirrups!"

There was no time to see if Maureen had done as he'd told her or not. He had to just hope that she had. As her horse began to fall, Longarm veered his own mount even closer to her and leaned over in the saddle. His arm shot out and wrapped around her waist. Maureen screamed as the horse tumbled out from under her, but Longarm's firm grip supported her and kept her from falling along with it. Using the pressure of his knees, he angled his own mount sharply away.

Maureen threw her arms around Longarm's neck and hung on for dear life. Her extra weight almost pulled him sideways out of the saddle, but then he managed to haul her up in front of him so that the burden was on the stallion instead. During the tricky maneuver, his arm had slid up on her body a little, so that his hand was cupping her right breast as he hung on tightly to her. Normally, having his hand full of soft, warm womanflesh was a damned nice turn of events, but at the moment Longarm didn't really have time to appreciate what he was feeling.

The exhausted stallion kept running, but its strength was almost gone. Now, carrying double, it slowed even more. Longarm heard the exultant whoops from the gang of cow thieves as they closed in.

"Keep your head down," Longarm grated in Maureen's ear. He used his heels to jab the black stallion and send it leaping forward. At this rate, the poor creature's heart was going to burst, but there was nothing Longarm could do about it. The edge of Moss City was less than a quarter of a mile away. They had to try for it.

He looked at the rustlers, then looked ahead again. Suddenly he spotted what looked like flames coming from one of the buildings on the left side of the road. Townspeople were running along the street, no doubt intending to form a bucket brigade to keep the blaze from spreading to other buildings. With so many potential witnesses, surely Coffee and his men would turn back, Longarm thought.

But the pursuers showed no sign of slacking off. Their rifles were still barking, and lead still whined around the heads of Longarm and Maureen. Longarm slammed his boots into the heaving sides of the stallion, driving it on through the last stretch of the trail that turned into the main street of Moss City. Suddenly, buildings were flashing past them, and Longarm knew they had reached the settlement.

The big black horse staggered and whinnied, and Longarm felt it starting to go out from under him. Just as he'd done when Coffee's gang shot the other horse, just as he'd told Maureen to do when her mount fell, he kicked loose from the stirrups and threw himself out of the saddle. The difference was that this time he had Maureen in his arms. His grip clamped firmly about her as they tumbled through the air and slammed into the dusty street.

The impact knocked them apart. Longarm rolled crazily through the dirt, unable to tell where Maureen was or what had happened to her. He was gasping for breath as he came up on his knees and put down his left hand to steady himself. Coffee and the other rustlers, half a dozen riders in all, were pouring into the town and thundering down the street toward Longarm. He reached for the Colt he'd grabbed away from Coffee, and was thankful that it had remained in his holster during his wild fall from the black stallion. He palmed out the gun and lifted it.

The building that was on fire was right across the street, he noticed, but he didn't have a chance to see what was going on before Coffee and the other riders swept toward him, yelling and firing. Longarm snapped a couple of shots at them and then threw himself behind a nearby water trough. *Damn*, he thought. The whole thing was coming full circle. This mess had started with him belly-down behind a water trough while folks shot at him. That time, he'd been in the dark about why somebody was trying to kill him, though. Now he knew good and well why Coffee and the others wanted him dead.

He hunkered there as bullets thudded into the thick wood of the trough, looking around as best he could for Maureen. He still hadn't seen her, and he hoped she'd picked herself up and scurried for cover.

In the light from the burning building, Longarm saw the rustlers throwing lead at the citizens who'd gathered to fight the blaze, driving them off the street. He spotted Tom Coffee on one of the rearing horses, and knew that the boss rustler had commandeered a mount from one of the men who'd been killed when Maureen made her play to rescue him.

Longarm fired at Coffee, but missed in the uncertain light. Coffee wheeled his horse and yelled, "Charge him! He can't get all of us!"

Son of a bitch! Longarm hadn't figured Coffee would be *this* stubborn. The man's leadership of the gang was at stake, though. It had been Coffee who had sent bushwhackers to kill him twice, Coffee who was ultimately responsible for the deaths of those men. Unless Longarm died, Coffee would never be able to retain the respect of his other men.

Longarm lifted himself enough to fire again as the rustlers brought their rearing mounts under control and sent them plunging across the street toward the water trough where he'd taken cover. Coffee was right about one thing—Longarm couldn't down all of them. He had already reloaded once, while he and Maureen were fleeing from the rustlers, and now his gun was almost empty again. There wouldn't be any chance to reload. In a matter of seconds, they would overrun his position and shoot him to ribbons.

But then a gun boomed across the street and one of the rustlers went flying from his saddle. A voice bellowed, "Nobody shoots up my town!"

Longarm looked up to see Marshal Frank Nemo striding out of the burning building, which Longarm could tell now was a livery stable. Nemo had his gun in his hand, and he fired coolly and calmly as he walked toward the rustlers, exhibiting the same brand of foolhardy courage he had displayed during the aborted bank robbery back in La Junta.

Using the momentary respite Nemo had given him, Longarm pulled fresh cartridges from his coat pocket and thumbed them into his Colt. He snapped the cylinder shut and lifted the .44. He and Nemo had Coffee's gang in a cross fire, and Longarm intended to make the most of it. He came up in a crouch and blazed away at the confused rustlers.

"Let's get out of here, Tom!" one of the men yelled frantically, but Coffee ignored him. Instead of heeding the warning, Coffee spurred his horse toward Longarm, firing his six-gun as he came on.

Longarm dropped to the side and rolled as Coffee's bullets

plunked into the water in the trough. He came up on one knee and leveled the Colt at the onrushing outlaw. A slug from Coffee's gun whipped past Longarm's ear, but then Longarm was pressing the trigger, feeling the butt of the revolver buck against his palm as the weapon blasted.

Longarm's bullet drove into Coffee's chest, sending him backward out of the saddle as if he had just run into a wall. The boss rustler bounced once as he hit the street, but then his now-riderless horse whirled around, panicked by the gunfire, and trampled over him in its flight. One of the iron-shod hooves thudded in the middle of Coffee's face, but Longarm figured the man didn't feel it. Coffee had been dead before he hit the ground.

Nemo had downed a couple more of the rustlers, leaving only two of them on horseback. As Longarm stood up, the surviving wide-loopers threw down their guns and thrust their arms into the air. "Don't shoot!" one of them yelped. "We give up!"

Longarm stalked toward them, the Colt held ready in his hand for instant use. Nemo came up on the other side of the rustlers, and he ordered, "Get down from those horses! I ought to shoot you bastards anyway, coming into my town like this and trying to gun down honest citizens." The marshal looked over at the man he had just helped and added in an exclamation of recognition, "Longarm!"

"Howdy, Marshal," Longarm said, keeping his pistol trained on the two rustlers as they dismounted nervously. "I was mighty glad to see you come out of that livery when you did. What happened there anyway?"

"A prisoner escaped and set the place on fire," Nemo replied curtly, and Longarm felt the blood in his veins turn to ice.

"A prisoner?" he repeated.

"Yeah. You may have heard of him—Walt Hudson."

"He's dead?" Longarm asked.

"I had to kill him." Nemo answered the question without

taking his eyes off his new prisoners. "You two march over there to the jail," he told them. "And don't try anything, or so help me I'll kill you."

Longarm believed him, and from the expressions on the faces of the two rustlers, they did too.

Longarm's brain was spinning. Obviously, he was too late to help Hudson, but Nemo would pay for what he had done. Longarm was going to have the truth about all this, once and for all.

At the moment, however, Nemo was taking the prisoners to jail and the citizens of Moss City were crowding around again, some wanting to see what had happened, others using buckets to throw water on the burning livery stable. There was a narrow alley on each side of the building, and that had helped keep the blaze from spreading so far. A few sparks had landed on neighboring roofs and started to smolder, but alert townies had scrambled up to the tops of the buildings and extinguished those fires in the making.

Longarm used the opportunity to check the fallen rustlers, including Tom Coffee. Coffee's face had been pounded into pulp by the stampeding horse, and he was stone cold dead, just as Longarm had thought. So was another of the rustlers, and the other two men were unconscious, passed out from their wounds. The local doctor could take a look at them if he wanted, but Longarm didn't expect either man to live.

He was just turning away from one of the sprawled figures in the street when Maureen came running from an alley and threw herself into his arms. "Are you all right, Longarm?" she asked urgently.

He managed a grin as he replied, "Why, I'm just fine. How about you?"

"I'm all right. I'll have some bumps and bruises from that fall, but nothing's broken and none of their shots hit me. I was never so scared in all my life, however."

"Me neither," Longarm told her, although truthfully he had

170

been in so many scrapes that he no longer remembered which one had been the most frightening. There was no point in telling Maureen that, though. Instead he folded her in his arms again and hugged her tightly. That was the best cure for what ailed both of them right now.

After a moment, Longarm put a hand under her chin and tilted her head back so that he could look down into her eyes. "You lied to me back yonder in Boulder," he said. "You didn't have any intention of staying behind while I came back here, did you?"

"Of course not," she answered without hesitation. "It was important for me to see this through to the end, you know that. Besides, if I hadn't followed you and heard that shooting, I wouldn't have been able to help you." She glanced toward where Coffee's corpse lay in the street and shuddered. "Why was Mr. Coffee trying to kill you? I thought you and he were friends."

"Oh, he claimed to like me, all right, even when he was about to shoot me. But him and his bunch have been wide-looping cattle—stealing them—and he thought I was on to their game. I wasn't, but it didn't make any difference to Coffee. He figured he'd be better off if I was dead."

"Then *he* was behind those ambush attempts, and not—"

Longarm shook his head to stop her from saying anything else about Nemo. He glanced over his shoulder at the jail, but the marshal of Moss City hadn't reappeared yet. Longarm said, "Where'd you learn to shoot like that anyway? You handled that rifle of yours like a professional."

"I told you there was a riding academy in Washington. There was a shooting range too. I have to admit it was . . . different shooting at a real person and not a paper target. I hope I never have to do that again. I would have helped you when we got here if I'd still had a gun. Since I didn't, I thought the best thing I could do would be to get out of the way."

"That was smart thinking," Longarm assured her. "When I

didn't see you in the street, I figured you'd found yourself a hidey-hole somewhere."

"Longarm . . ." Maureen's voice dropped a little. "What about Nemo? And Walt?"

Longarm had been wishing he didn't have to tell Maureen what had happened, since a friendship had sprung up between her and the horse rancher from Kansas. But there was no getting around it, so he said, "Hudson's in that burning building over there. Nemo killed him."

Maureen's fingers clutched at his arms. "No! He can't have done that!"

"He did," Longarm said with a bleak nod. "But it's all over, Maureen. The hell with evidence or doing things right and proper. I'm taking that son of a bitch down, even if he did help me against Coffee and his bunch."

"What are you going to do?"

Before Longarm could answer, a familiar voice called in surprise, "Mrs. Paige? Is that you?"

Longarm turned, sliding his left arm around Maureen's shoulders so that his right hand would be free. They faced Nemo as the renegade lawman strode across the street toward them. The flames consuming the livery stable had died down some by now, but they still cast enough light for Longarm to see the puzzled frown on Nemo's face.

The marshal came to a stop about ten feet from them and hooked his thumbs in his gunbelt, looking a lot more casual than he had to be feeling right about now. He said, "Well, it was a big enough surprise seeing you here again, Longarm, but I thought the lady was going back East."

"Plans get changed, Nemo," Longarm said brusquely.

Nemo's frowned deepened. "I swear, you're starting to sound a mite unfriendly. I don't like to remind a man of a favor I've done him, but those boys who chased you into town would've killed you if I hadn't stepped in. You might do well to remember that, Longarm."

172

"Oh, I remember it, all right, and I appreciate the help. But that doesn't change the facts. You and me still got some things to hash out, Nemo."

"Like what?" the marshal asked coolly.

"Like Walt Hudson." Longarm's voice was hard and blunt.

Nemo stiffened slightly. "I told you what happened. The old gent who runs the livery stable will confirm my story. Hudson escaped from jail and ran down to the stable to steal a horse for his getaway. I followed and had to shoot him when he wouldn't stop. Or don't you believe me?"

Longarm didn't respond to Nemo's sally right away. He said to Maureen, "You'd best step over there onto the boardwalk, out of the way."

"Are you sure?" she asked.

"I'm sure," he told her.

He kept an eye on Nemo as Maureen walked quickly out of the line of fire. There was no telling when the marshal would make his move. Evidently, though, Nemo wasn't ready to crack just yet, because he said loudly, "What's wrong, Longarm? I've told you the truth. If you're calling me a liar, you'd better have a damn good reason to back it up."

Longarm glanced at the crowd of townspeople who were turning to look at them, their attention drawn by Nemo's loud comments. The marshal was trying to get the townies on his side, so that if Longarm drew, Nemo would look justified in gunning him.

Longarm saw some familiar faces in that crowd, though—Mama and Papa Frederickson, Sampson the mayor, and several more of the businessmen who had come calling on Longarm at the Moss City Inn a few days earlier and asked him to do something about Nemo. He called out, "You people wanted the truth about your lawman! Well, I'll give you the truth—Frank Nemo's a cold-blooded killer! The prisoner he murdered tonight was no criminal. Walt Hudson was working for me!"

The citizens stirred and muttered among themselves. Many

173

of them were already unhappy with Frank Nemo, and they were a receptive audience for Longarm's accusations. But they fell back a step, flinching involuntarily, when Nemo swung toward them and glared, his face a stony mask.

"If you believe that, you're crazy!" Nemo said. "This fella's power must've gone to his head. He figures since he's a federal lawman he can say any damn thing he pleases and get away with it!"

"You're a fine one to talk about power going to somebody's head, Nemo," Longarm snapped. "You've been using your power to get away with murder ever since you left Missouri. What'd you call yourself back there? Were you still Frank Nemo, or did you use the name Arronax—maybe even Ned Land! How about it?"

Nemo's eyes widened, and Longarm knew that the references to Verne's novel had surprised him. The big deputy forged on, wanting to press any advantage he might have. He said, "Never mind, I reckon I know why you chose the name. The captain in the story said it himself—'Nemo' means 'nothing.' And that's what you are, mister. Nothing."

Nemo's voice quivered with rage as he said, "You son of a bitch. You get out of my town and don't ever come back. Get out of my town or I'll kill you!"

"I ain't a prisoner, and I ain't escaping. You'll have to do it face to face, Nemo."

"Shut up!" Nemo cried. "Shut up, damn you!" He looked at the townspeople and gestured savagely toward Longarm. "Some of you get him! Ride him out of town on a rail!"

No one budged.

Except toward the rear of the crowd, where someone suddenly yelled, "Hey, there's somebody else coming out of the stable!"

That made everybody jerk around in surprise, including Longarm and Nemo. Along with everyone else, they saw the figure stumbling out of the ruined barn. Behind the man, the roof of the structure finally gave way and crashed in, causing the flames to leap higher once more and sparks to cascade skyward into the black night.

"Longarm . . . !" the man called in a feeble voice.

It was Walt Hudson.

The rancher was badly burned and covered with soot and ashes, and the left side of his shirt was dark and sodden with blood. He swayed, and would have fallen if Papa Frederickson had not lunged out to catch hold of his arm with a strong hand. More men closed around him to support him, and Maureen cried, "Walt!" as she ran across the street to join them.

Through lips cracked and blackened by the flames, Hudson said loudly, "Nemo . . . Nemo's lying! He . . . he set the fire. He's a . . . killer, just like Longarm . . . said."

Nemo turned on his heel and stalked toward him, shouting, "Shut up, you son of a bitch! What's wrong with you people? You're not going to take the word of an outlaw, are you? This man stole a fortune in bonds!"

"A fortune that you . . . wanted," accused Hudson. Longarm wasn't sure where he'd gotten the strength to hold up through the ordeal he had endured, but he was glad that Hudson had survived the inferno in the barn. The injured rancher went on. "There weren't really . . . any bonds. But Nemo thought there was, and he said . . . he'd let me go if . . . if I paid him off. He . . . he's done it before . . . told his prisoners he'd pretend to . . . to kill them . . . then let them go and kill somebody else to take their place."

That was it, Longarm thought. Nemo was a crook as well as a killer. That was the last piece of the puzzle.

But not quite. Hudson groaned, then said, "But he's crazy . . . took the money . . . killed 'em anyway."

"You goddamn liar!" Nemo screamed. His hand flashed toward the pistol on his hip.

175

"Nemo!" shouted Longarm. The crowd was closing ranks around Hudson to keep him from being hurt any more, but if Nemo drew on them, innocent people could still get killed. Longarm didn't want that. There had been enough killing.

Well, almost.

Nemo spun toward Longarm, the gun sliding whisper-smooth from its holster, the barrel tipping up. Nemo's finger tightened on the trigger.

Longarm's .44 was in his hand again and flame geysered from its muzzle an instant before Nemo fired. The reports were so close together they almost sounded like one shot. Longarm felt the wind of Nemo's slug fanning his face, but the renegade marshal's shot was still a clean miss.

The honest lawman's bullet slammed into Nemo's chest, lifting him and knocking him backward as it bored into his body. Nemo crashed to the ground on his back, his arms outflung, the pistol slipping from his fingers to thud into the dirt.

A few quick, long-legged strides covered the distance between Longarm and Nemo, and Longarm kicked the fallen gun well out of Nemo's reach. Nemo's eyes were open, and his mouth worked soundlessly as he stared up at Longarm. A thin trickle of blood came from his lips.

Longarm looked down at the man for a moment, then said, "Well, you ain't going twenty thousand leagues under the sea, Nemo. I reckon six feet under the ground'll have to do you."

The eyes of the man who called himself Frank Nemo turned glassy in death.

Longarm holstered his gun and went to join Maureen and Walt Hudson, who was grinning crookedly at him despite the injuries he'd suffered. "All . . . over . . . ain't it?" Hudson asked.

"All over," Longarm agreed. "Now come on, folks, let's get this man to a doctor!"

The crowd moved down the street toward the local physician's office, leaving Frank Nemo sprawled in the street. The livery barn continued burning, sending sparks spiraling up into the sky, where they glowed for a few seconds and then winked out.

Chapter 15

Longarm brushed a hand at the fly or whatever it was that was tickling his ear, then worked his head down deeper in the pillow. The bed in this room in the Moss City Inn was sinfully soft, and he intended to stay there a while longer, no matter how late in the morning it was getting. He hadn't gotten to bed until well after midnight the night before, what with making sure that Hudson was patched up properly and getting the undertaker to deal with Nemo, Coffee, and the other dead men. He still had some catching up to do on his sleep.

But that damned fly was an insistent little bastard, hopping down the line of his jaw and onto his chest. He turned over and pushed the sheet back a little, brushing at the annoyance again.

It wasn't a fly he shooed away, though. His fingers touched soft, silky hair. That was what had been tickling him, he realized as he came more fully awake.

Then something hot and wet trailed through the mat of hair on his chest and circled around his left nipple. Longarm grinned but kept his eyes closed as someone pushed the sheet on down his body, revealing the fact that he'd taken off his long underwear before coming to bed.

"Lordy, I must still be asleep, because I'm sure dreaming," he announced.

"Ssshhh," said a soft voice. A second later, warm lips traced a path down his belly. Slender fingers played over his thighs, gripping and kneading his muscles with surprising strength. He felt that silky hair spreading out over his groin as his visitor moved her mouth closer to the rapidly stiffening length of his manhood.

Another moment passed, a maddening interval while those warm, moist lips lifted away from his belly. Then they closed around his shaft, and a fervent sigh escaped from Longarm's throat. He couldn't take lying there with his eyes closed any longer, so he opened them and lifted his head, propping the pillow under it so that he could watch as Maureen Paige nuzzled and suckled his throbbing flesh. She was every bit as naked as he was, and he spotted her clothes draped over the back of a chair near the bed. Obviously, she had decided that he'd slept late enough.

Under the circumstances, he had to agree with her, no matter how late it had been the night before when he went to sleep.

She had her back half-turned toward him as she knelt beside him on the bed, and it was easy for him to reach up between her legs and cup his hand over the thatch of red hair covering her mound. She moaned deep in her throat and sucked harder as he squeezed lightly. His thumb slipped easily into her as he caressed the folds of wet, hot flesh.

Her tongue circled and swooped, and the tip of it teased the opening at the end of his shaft. Longarm felt the need boiling up inside him and knew that he couldn't withstand much more of this delicious torment. He grasped Maureen's shoulders, tugging gently and pulling her mouth up to his. He slid his hands down to her hips and lifted her, poising her over him and then lowering her slowly. With a thrust of his hips, he slid into her, their bodies merging until the red hair of her triangle was mashed hard against his crotch. She made little sounds of desire as her hips began working back and forth.

179

The movements were small but intense. "Oh, God, you fill me up so!" she whispered.

Longarm cupped a hand behind her head, his fingers buried deep within the thick red hair. He kissed her again, sending his tongue between her parted lips. His other hand massaged the small of her back and then trailed down to the swell of her buttocks and the cleft between them. Her breasts were flattened against his chest as she lay atop him, the erect nipples prodding him urgently. He braced himself and drove even deeper inside her.

Time meant nothing. Longarm could never be sure how much of it passed while they made love, but finally neither of them could deny themselves any longer. Maureen sat up, resting the palms of her hands on his chest, and pumped her hips back and forth wildly as she rode him. Longarm met her thrust for thrust, giving as good as he got, until at last she froze stock still except for a series of tiny tremors that ran through her. His climax washed over him at the same time, sending scalding liquid fire out of him and into her. Maureen gave a huge shudder that seemed to reach into her very core, then collapsed on top of him, utterly sated and breathless.

Longarm was a mite out of breath himself.

When she could talk again without gasping, Maureen said, "That was wonderful, Longarm. I hope you don't mind that I woke you up."

"Not hardly," he chuckled.

"I . . . I wanted this morning to be special."

Longarm sensed there was some extra meaning behind her words. He looked at her and said, "This is so long, isn't it?"

"I'm afraid so." Maureen rolled off him and sat up, looking a little uncomfortable now. "I hope you're not upset, and I hope you don't think I'm some sort of . . . some sort of cheap woman. But you'll be going back to Denver so that you can report to Marshal Vail, won't you?"

"I'll ride out today," Longarm told her gently.

"And Walt has asked me to stay here in Moss City until he's recuperated from his injuries enough to travel. He's anxious to get back to his ranch, and I thought I'd go with him to make sure that he gets there safely."

"Sounds like a good idea," Longarm said. "You're a mighty capable woman, Maureen. I reckon you'll take good care of ol' Walt."

"I might stay on his ranch for a while after we get there too, before I go back East. Just to make sure everything is all right, you understand."

Longarm nodded solemnly. "The whole thing sounds fine by me."

She frowned at him for a few seconds, then punched him lightly on the arm. "You could be a little upset about it, you know," she said. "You don't have to be quite so damned understanding."

Longarm scooted into a sitting position and held up his hands in mock surrender. "No offense, Maureen, but I'm old enough to know that most things don't last, no matter how good they are. Folks need to just enjoy the good times while they've got 'em. That's what I try to do."

She leaned closer to him. "And despite all the trouble, there were some good times, weren't there?"

"Damned good times, especially once you thawed out a mite."

"Thawed out?" She punched him again. "I'll show you just how thawed out I am, Deputy Long!" She kissed him again as he brought his hands up to caress her breasts.

"That's what I was counting on . . ." Longarm murmured.

"What I don't understand is why Nemo even notified the authorities in the first place if he was planning all along to kill his prisoners," Maureen said.

She and Longarm were sitting in the room at the local doctor's house where Walt Hudson was resting in bed. Hudson was sitting up, revealing the layers of bandages wrapped around his midsection. His face and hands were smeared with grease to relieve the pain of the burns he had suffered in the livery stable.

Longarm had a cheroot going. He puffed on it contentedly for a moment, then said, "Nemo figured he was smarter than everybody else. That kind usually does. Calling in federal officers and then killing the prisoners before they got there was part of the game to him. Besides, he had to keep up his image as a respectable lawman for the townspeople in the places he worked, and that's what a real marshal would've done. And it gave him some extra leverage with the prisoners too. He could tell 'em that he'd already wired the federal marshal's office, and if they didn't come up with the money he wanted, he'd just go ahead and turn them in."

"But he had to realize that sooner or later someone would notice how his prisoners kept winding up dead," Maureen protested. "Just like you did, Longarm."

The big deputy shrugged. "A man like Nemo's got so much arrogance in him, it's got to come out somehow."

"Longarm's right," Hudson put in. He still sounded a little weak, but his condition was already improving. The doctor said that he had the constitution of a horse, and Hudson intended to prove that was correct. He went on. "Nemo had me dead to rights, but when he heard all the shooting going on in the street, he must've decided not to waste a bullet finishing me off. He figured the fire would do that. So he left me in there and went out to see what was going on."

"Good thing for me," Longarm said. "I reckon he had a sense of duty, even if it was all twisted out of shape. He wasn't going to stand by and let Coffee's bunch shoot up the town—and me."

"When I came to, I knew I had to get out before the roof came down, so I managed to stand up and start stumbling toward the front of the barn." Hudson shivered. "I don't want to ever go through something like that again. I reckon I know what hell looks like now."

"Nemo does, that's for damned sure," Longarm said. He put his hands on his knees and pushed himself to his feet. "I reckon I'd better be riding. My boss's probably getting a mite anxious to find out what happened up here." He couldn't shake hands with Hudson, considering how the rancher's hands were burned, so he settled for slapping him lightly on the shoulder. "So long, Walt. Sorry I got you into this mess."

"Shoot, Longarm, if it wasn't for you, I'd've barged in here and got myself killed for sure when I braced Nemo." Hudson sighed. "At least Ellen and Maureen's husband and all the other folks Nemo murdered have been avenged. That's worth something."

"It's worth a great deal," Maureen said, "but it's even better knowing that Nemo won't put anyone else through the misery he put us through."

Longarm nodded. "You two take care of each other, you hear. You've both got some forgetting to do, and I reckon the best way to do that is to have something to look forward to." He grinned, sketched a casual salute to Maureen and Hudson, and left the doctor's house.

The townspeople had given him a horse, and they were already at work rebuilding old Josh's stable. The citizens of Moss City were a pretty good bunch of folks, Longarm thought as he swung up into the saddle and turned the horse's nose toward Denver. But he was still glad to be leaving. As he had told Maureen and Hudson, he had some things to look forward to himself. One of them was giving his report to Billy Vail and closing the file on this bizarre case.

And then there was that sweet-looking library gal . . . What was her name? Mary Alice? Longarm thought that sounded right. Maybe he'd get her to show him where to find the Jules Verne books again. It was sort of dark and quiet back there in those shelves, and maybe he'd try to steal a kiss or two . . .

Longarm grinned and jogged the horse into a trot.

Watch for

LONGARM AND THE HIGH ROLLERS

186th novel in the bold LONGARM series
from Jove

Coming in June!